APOLOGIES FORTHCOMING

Xujun Eberlein

Livingston Press
The University of West Alabama

ACKNOWLEDGEMENTS

Several stories in this collection have been previously published, sometimes in slightly different form, in the following magazines: "Pivot Point" in *AGNI 62* (Fall 2005); "Men Don't Apologize" in *Night Train* (Spring 2005); "Watch the Thrill" in *Stand* (UK, Fall 2004) and *Meridian* (Fall/ Winter 2004); "Disciple of the Masses" in *StoryQuarterly 40* (October 2004) with the title "Goldbach's Conjecture"; "The Randomness of Love" in *The Saint Ann's Review* (Summer/Fall 2004); "Snow Line" in *Cottonwood* (Fall 2003) and *Kwani* (Kenya, Fall 2003); "Second Encounter" in *Thought Magazine* (June 2003) and *Paumanok Review* (Winter 2004). The lines of poetry quoted in "Snow Line" (except page 16) are my translation of poems from a friend, Yo Xiaosu, published with permission. The poem quoted on page 16 is translated from "Trees" (1939) by poet Ai Qing (1910-1996).

TABLE OF CONTENTS

I deeply appreciate the generosity of Mr. Wu Fan, a great Chinese artist, and his family for allowing me to reprint three of his block prints as insets in this volume. The opening story, "Snow Line," alludes to "Dandelion," which gained Mr. Wu Fan an international reputation in early 1960s, but also caused him great misery during the Cultural Revolution. I am honored that my story shares space with this masterpiece of artwork.

APOLOGIES FORTHCOMING

SNOW LINE

1.

Shiao Su had searched every inch of his room, under the bed, under his roommates' beds, under the piles of dirty laundry, in every drawer of his desk, between the pages of every textbook, but still couldn't find what he was looking for. For a moment he even doubted if it had ever existed.

The class bell was already ringing as he dragged himself toward the Economics Department Building, wincing when the forgotten cigarette burned his fingers. The bright sunshine and gentle breeze of May failed to soothe him. From the other side of the high brick wall that separated the campus and an elementary school, clear voices of children reading their textbooks surmounted the wall with the breeze:

> "I—love—Beijing—Tian-an-men
> Above it—the sun—is—rising . . ."

The uninformed innocent voices irritated him; that was the same text he had read in elementary school. There seemed no evidence that this was already the 1980s. In the distance, at the entrance of this largest university in southwest China, stood a lime-white, larger-than-life-size statue of Chairman Mao, one arm raised, beckoning you to enter the campus. There the statue had stood for the decade during which the university, like all others in the nation, was closed. Since the university reopened three years ago, Shiao Su had heard of similar statues quietly disappearing from some campuses farther east. An eastern poet had even begun to use, ever so shyly, the word "love" without reference to a political symbol. But for some reason the west seemed always behind the east in China, just as the sun always arrives later.

Shiao Su remained in this distracted state of mind through his economics classes until late morning, toward the end of his math class. The professor was a skinny man of average height in his early 40s, only a couple of years older than the oldest students in the class, the very first admitted after the decade-long Cultural Revolution. There had been an exam the day before and, as was conventional, the professor had just read the names of students who scored above 90 in the test. His level voice stirred up some excitement and some disappointment in the classroom. Shiao Su did not hear his name and he stared at the professor's thick glasses, his eyes perplexed behind his own glasses.

Suddenly, the professor's voice became animated. "Now I want to read you the best answer sheet I've ever seen!" This unexpected move stilled the class of 32 men and women. This was not part of convention. Students in the front rows could see that the pages in the professor's hand were upside down and he was looking at the wrong side. He walked to the front edge of the raised dais and read with as much gusto as his thin chest would allow:

> *"First seeing you as in fog*
> *Across a drifting earth, longing your graceful figure*

Is this a wild wish?
I instantly utter—
Be my wife!"

He waved one arm to the audience like a flag as he yelled out "Be my wife," receiving a few suppressed chuckles. A student raised his hand. The professor impatiently permitted his question.

"Be my wife?" the young man asked in a baffled tone. "That's a solution to the math test?" The whole class burst into an uproarious laughter.

The professor raised his palm for silence.

"This is poetry, understand? Poetry! The twin-brother of mathematics!" Then he sighed, "I have not seen a real poem in ages." Before the class calmed completely he again engaged himself in the passionate reading:

"The sun sets, highlighting a mountain peak
On the edge of the green shaded cliff
I throw down a bouquet
The echo says—
Be my wife!"

Another wave of laughter rolled across the classroom but the professor kept reading:

"The fond poet sleeps in a little log house
Wolves cry deep in the woods
Only the moon bends down, recognizing
Each fresh character on the grassy hill—
Be my wife! . . ."

The women students did not join in the laughter. As in any science and engineering classes, they were a small minority. All seven lowered their heads to hide moist eyes.

Shiao Su sat motionlessly, his long back up straight, his glasses glimmering. He was totally awake. Only now did he understand why he could not find the draft of his first poem, and why his name was not in the top score list as it had often been. As the professor kept on, Shiao Su hoped the author's name might not be revealed.

When the last words of the poem hit the floor with the sounds of brass cymbals, the laughter finally died down. In the fresh silence the bell rang. The professor collected his papers and walked out of the classroom; the women students hurriedly followed.

Behind them, a shrill male voice suddenly broke into a solo of a popular, though long-forbidden, folk song:

"If you wanna be a bride,
Don't be another's—"

All but one man, old and young, picked up the lyrics in one united tone:

"You just gotta be mine!"

Then, pounding their hands on desks, they shouted out as one "Be my wife," breaking out once again into uncontrolled laughter.

For several nights in a row various handwritten copies of Shiao Su's maiden poem, "Golden Bell," quietly passed from room to room in the women students' dorm. In some rooms candles burned into the small hours after the lights-off bell, as girls concentrated on copying the poem by hand:

". . . The old captain died; the ocean was his life
His ship with proudest mast— now passed on to me
I sail tomorrow, faraway
My heart hides the words—
Be my wife!

Holding sleeves of dawn I float
Put your beloved orchid on the windowsill
Your cat standing on the headboard
I stoop to ask—
Be my wife!

Where will the sampan drift?
Finally stranding at a river oasis
Frightened, my first kiss to you
I murmur—
Be my wife!

Comes autumn, the rice turns gold
Reluctantly, geese part from the lake
Long chasing remnants of sunset clouds
My voice getting hoarse—
Be my wife!"

The poem fell into the hands of a student Party member from the countryside. Though she angrily condemned the "yellow poem," she kept reading. The girl who had shown it to her panicked and tried to grab the paper back; the Party member held it tightly. Rumor was that after that, she hand-copied the entire poem and hid it in her locked drawer, offering a revision for the other girl's copy: "How about changing 'be my wife' to 'be my comrade'?" The other girl did not dare protest.

So that was how the pointy tip of the awl emerged from the pocket. Shiao Su became a well-known lyric poet literally overnight. In the next few months his name constantly hung on the lips of female university students all over Sichuan Province. Despite the Party's rule "no talk of love on campus" that had caused the math professor to be denounced after the fateful class, a few brave girls attempted to contact Shiao Su. They were too late: the poem had already reached its mark. In the circulation of "Golden Bell" there were many variations. Incidentally, or perhaps intentionally, most of them did not have the ending stanza:

> *"Says she, my response—*
> *Strawberry, mud, olives and baby deer"*

2.

As flower fragrance graced the summer air of Chengdu, hand copies and mimeographs of Shiao Su's poetry made their way to other universities and the public. His newly discovered talent resurrected his old Pa's dead hope for him to become a dragon, while bothering his wife-to-be, Qian-qian, with reason.

One Sunday morning when Shiao Su and Qian-qian were enjoying their weekend together, without warning a small crowd of young women came to Shiao Su's house, or more precisely his parents' house, located in downtown of Chengdu, a half-hour bicycle's ride from the campus. Shiao Su politely let them in, turning around only to find that Qian-qian had disappeared. The curtain between his bedroom and the small living room swayed in the wind brought in by the uninvited guests. After introducing themselves as "literary youths," the girls started pouring out questions, such as, "How did you start writing poems as a science student?" or "What's the purpose of your writing?" He noticed some of them kept eyeing the swaying curtain and he wondered what Qian-qian was doing behind it.

Shiao Su lit a cigarette and sat quietly smoking. In the curling smoke and an invisible fog of unfamiliar perfume, he felt a slight headache caused by the questions. Once he had written a foreword to his poetry: "No matter what the topic, when I give up studying its essence, I find myself unspeakably happy and relaxed." Another time, several men from the Chinese Literature Department had a big debate about his motivation for writing. They finally reached an agreement that writing poems "is the best way to radiate outward the strength of his life." The fact that Shiao Su's academic scores were good, and that he was also a key member of the university's track and field team, were excluded from his "strength." They came to tell him their conclusion and wanted to know what he thought about it. He conveniently wrote two lines on the back of a cigarette pack as the answer: "*The value of all arguments / Merely worth a glowing cigarette butt.*"

But the playful disdain for the rational was a trick that Shiao Su could only perform on men. In his 25 years of life he had not learnt how to deal with women, especially rational women. He had no alternative but to answer, "Ah, I wrote just for fun."

His words touched off a wave of dissatisfied tongue-clicking, but another curious question surfaced at that moment. "Could we see her?" one pretty girl asked with a shy smile. It looked like the questions had held her for quite a while. Shiao Su was softened by her hopeful eyes but he listened to Qian-qian's heart beating behind the curtain. He shook his head and said, "She's not here. Maybe next time?"

Another girl was encouraged by this and asked for their love story. When she heard that the couple was introduced by a matchmaker friend, and that Qian-qian was a common government employee, not a college student, and only 21 years old, the girl's shining eyes dimmed a little. At this point Shiao Su knew that the peak of their enthusiasm had passed. A note of disappointment echoed silently between the host and the guests.

Not until almost an hour later did Qian-qian dare to lift the curtain. Eyeing the emptied living room, her pink cheeks pouted a little and she mumbled, "Could you stop mixing with those *literary* women?"

"Okay my little deer," Shiao Su replied and placed a light kiss on her youthful lips. She dodged away from his next attempt and warned with a childish anger:

"Be careful, your mother is back!"

As a punishment to his "mixing" with other girls, Qian-qian ordered Shiao Su to accompany her to the farmers' market. Carrying Qian-qian on his bike's handlebars, Shiao Su rode through the twisting alleys, where there were no traffic police, to arrive at the West Suburb Bridge farmers' market.

Before Shiao Su locked up the bike Qian-qian was already off, bouncing along the gravel road. Her slickers kicked the small stones up and away; she was humming a children's song. Ahead of her, wicker and bamboo baskets of green, yellow, and white vegetables arrayed with purple, blue, pink and red flowers, all lined up on both sides of the road. Farmers, both women and men, cried out under the golden sun, "Come on here, mine's selling cheap!"

It took Shiao Su a while to move his gaze away from Qian-qian as she sunk into the crowded market. Looking around, his eyes caught a sign, "Modern Art Gallery." He had heard that this was the first private gallery in Chengdu.

He walked into the small, empty hall. Oil and water paintings of all sizes were arranged artfully on three white walls. A young man wearing a colorfully stained canvas apron greeted him so warmly that Shiao Su was a little flustered; he was used to the salesclerks' rude yelling in the government-run stores.

Shiao Su perused the walls, occasionally making a stop. Something caught his attention in a quiet corner. He glanced at it, walked past it, and came back to it. He looked closer and lightning struck.

Under a small oil painting were a few lines of his poem written in delicate script of small characters:

> *Not a man walking toward me*
> *Not a bundle of familiar sunrays*
> *Only a land of wild flowers*
> *Accompany me*
> *In dusk with no wind*
> *Begin a trek with no reason*

He looked at the oil painting with surprise and pleasure. He had been enjoying echoes from his audience; but he had never expected to receive a message from a different form of art. The oil painting was titled "Balang Mountains," with a cool color bias in a purple keynote. Clusters of mysterious flowers and open grounds between wild bushes appeared misty and hazy. From the haziness rose a rich autumn mountain smell, inexplicably touching. Shiao Su let out a sigh; the genuine mood in the painting erased any pretentiousness he perceived in his poem.

The painting was signed "Dandelion." So oil painters also use pen names? Shiao Su thought curiously. He stood in front of "Balang Mountains" for quite a while before he walked away to look at other paintings. Then he came back again.

"Peek-a-boo! I just knew you would be here." Qian-qian's giggles startled him. He shushed her and took over a full basket of produce from her hand. For a split second, a question mark flickered in Qian-qian's eyes. She went closer to the painting and looked at the artist's name.

"That's a girl's name — I swear to Chairman Mao," she commented as they walked out of the gallery together.

"Chairman Mao is dead," Shiao Su responded with a reassuring smile, his free arm holding her smooth shoulder. He did not think more explanation was needed, as she was unlikely to have recognized his poem. In the trip home Qian-qian sat on the rear carrier kicking the wheel all the way, while Shiao Su could not stop contemplating the wild Balang Mountains and the mysterious purple mist, vaguely feeling its seductive power.

That evening Qian-qian cooked a banquet for the family, including Shiao Su's favorite dishes, "Sea Cucumbers Braised in Brown Sauce" and "Tingling Hot Tofu." The plate of "Kong-pao Chicken" was a "wine dish" for Shiao Su's father, and the "Sand-pot of Fish Head" was for his mother. Shiao Su, usually quiet and a light eater, opened up both his stomach and mouth, making everyone chuckle over the dinner table. Whatever the reason, he was in an excellent mood and did not bother to analyze it.

3.

As Shiao Su's poems grew increasingly popular, the enticement of seeing them properly printed and bound also increased. However, his submissions to national and local literary magazines were like stones sinking into the sea. The few that ever returned rejection slips had brief comments such as "unhealthy sentimentalism of the petty bourgeoisie," "obscure words nobody can understand," or "mist poems do not suit Chinese readers."

His father tried to help by connecting him with an editor friend. Uncle Jin was the chief editor of *Sichuan Youth*, a government-run political magazine. The magazine had newly opened a poetry section. In his desperation Shiao Su set out to see Uncle Jin. "You have talent, truly, you have talent," Uncle Jin said encouragingly. "I plan to use two of your poems. But," he paused and looked apologetically at Shiao Su, "as you know, this is the Party's magazine. You'll have to make several corrections here."

Uncle Jin went on for the particular corrections, including the replacement of the word "love" with "revolutionary affection." Shiao Su was too well mannered to refuse and agreed to do what Uncle Jin asked. He just hoped that Dandelion, whoever she was, did not read this magazine. After he walked out he never returned.

The only choice left was to publish himself. This was an unheard of concept to Chinese in the early '80s; but the future dragons and tigers in Shiao Su's economics class were not afraid to set precedents with unknown concepts. They formed a well-conceived plan, including applying for the imprimatur, designing the book cover, printing the book, and marketing it. All these steps involved backdoors; but who in this class did not have a few connections?

Shiao Su's assignment was to get the book of his poetry, *Black Snow*, printed in a street-run printing shop. He was told he must meet the contact there in after-hours and avoid the shop manager. The contact's name was Yue Zhu.

When Shiao Su arrived at the shabby printing shop it was dusk. In the air mixed with mold and the smell of oil ink, under bright fluorescent lights he saw the side of a tall girl standing alone and working on a type board. Her off-white cotton shirt and matching skirt were as simple as elegance. A green silk ribbon loosely flowing with her waterfall, shoulder-length hair, made him wonder how the ribbon could be so loose and still stay, as though it were a strand of her hair.

The green ribbon danced away; their eyes met. He was unprepared to see a pair of calmly intelligent eyes. She nodded to him with a serene smile as if he was a long-time acquaintance. "Hi. I'll be finishing in a moment," she said softly while her hands kept up swift movements.

Shiao Su walked closer and saw she was picking the small lead characters from the type case and placing them into a stereotype board. In front of her, the layout of a newspaper page was nearly finished. With effort he recognized the reversed characters that formed the headlines: *Uphold the Party's leadership! Uphold the socialist road! Uphold proletarian dictatorship! Uphold Marxism, Leninism, and Mao Zedong Thought!* The same proclamation for the "four upholds" in all newspapers every day.

"Does this work bore you?" The question slipping out of his lips made him gasp. He did not even know her!

Yue Zhu did not stop her deft hands, nor lift up her eyes. He could only hear her calm voice: "I don't think when I am working."

Shiao Su shut up and walked away a few steps to look around. There were no windows in the rather large, storage-room like workshop. On the facing white wall that was free from equipment and supply boxes was a large manual timesheet with dates, names and red checks and crosses. Beside it was a framed space labeled "Study Gains," the words that were so familiar and so remote at the same time. In the framed space, notebook-size pages lined up tidily like soldiers in parade, except one that was not hung well and slightly tilted. Without another look, he knew exactly what was written on the pages: the workers' reiteration of what they had gained after studying Chairman Mao's works. And every page had more or less the same words, the words that everyone wrote but no one read. The only tiny variation within this tidy space was that lone tilted page.

Shiao Su suddenly missed the vast track fields and the modern library building of his campus. He looked at Yue Zhu again and could not put together her elegant figure and calm demeanor with this workshop where no daylight could come in. He felt gratitude when Yue Zhu led him out.

Shiao Su followed Yue Zhu to the end of the hallway along the shop's wall outside. She opened a door and let him in.

He instantly saw this was actually a corner of the workshop they had just walked out of, with cardboard walls separating this small "room" from the rest of the shop. A room big enough to handle a few pieces of simple furniture: a single bed with a bamboo bookshelf as its end, a small square rosewood tea table, and a bench. There was even a small window on one side of the real wall; it looked as though it had been chiseled out by hand as an afterthought. A long, quaint, wooden *Zheng* sat horizontally in front of the window; above it hung a large basin of wild ferns. A mountain soil smell spread out of the ferns.

"You live *here?*" Shiao Su asked with genuine surprise. He wondered how many more surprises Yue Zhu was going to give him tonight.

"Ah — my father's apartment is as small as this one. Besides, not too bad to have my own place." Yue Zhu smiled.

"Your father . . ." Shiao Su stopped in the middle of the question as his sight was caught by a woodcut print on one wall. A little girl, five or six years old, kneeled in a meadow blowing a dandelion. He could not believe his eyes.

" . . . is Lord Yue!" he cried out. Fragments of tales about the legendary artist and his family flashed through his memory. Lord Yue won a golden medal for his woodcut "Dandelion" in a world art competition in the '60s; Red Guards raided his big house and seized the medal during the Cultural

Revolution; after many public denunciations Lord Yue and his wife turned on the gas stove during a dark winter night; the teenage daughter rescued the father but lost her mother forever . . .

Yue Zhu ignored his exclamation. "Don't you want to talk about your poetry book?" she asked.

"Yes, but wait, why don't you apply for the College of Fine Arts?" Shiao Su could not stop his tongue. That's the only way for her to get out this printing shop, he thought.

Yue Zhu smiled placidly. "I did and I was admitted. But my father does not want me to be an artist."

Shiao Su's next question hung up in the middle of the air. He was quiet for a few seconds.

"I'm really sorry," he murmured at last.

Yue Zhu laughed softly. "Why, this is nothing. Not too bad to be a worker and to live on my own wages." She paused, and then added: "It wasn't easy to get this job, you know."

Shiao Su was again silenced. Countless young people their age had come back from the countryside at the end of the Cultural Revolution, and failed to pass the entrance exams for college. They were now a huge unemployment force that had been classified by the government as waiting-for-employment youths. Yue Zhu and he should feel lucky . . . but was she really lucky?

The remaining glow of the setting sun spilled onto the windowsill and the little square table. Yue Zhu infused a purple-sand pot of jasmine tea, and sat down on the edge of the bed. The two sat by the table sipping tea and talked about the details of the printing process of *Black Snow*. In the fragrant air of tea, ferns and sunrays, Shiao Su's soul slowly returned to tranquility.

"Your room is like a fairy tale," he commented before leaving. "Where did you buy that? Some kind of fern? I've never seen it in the flower markets."

"I dug it from the mountains."

"Which mountains? Balang?"

Yue Zhu apparently did not expect this. She glanced at him and ruminated.

He hesitated, but could not help asking: "Did you go there alone?"

"It's a place of wild soil and wild water. A place for going alone."

"I know it's not a tourist place. But could you please be our guide? My class is organizing an autumn outing and I want to go there." Then he added more firmly, "We are going there."

She did not answer immediately. He followed her pondering eyes to the quaint instrument, long and narrow, tapered from one carved end to the other. Threads of long metal-wound silk strings covered its top. Behind the instrument was a music stand with a closed book titled *Classic Zheng Music*. He wondered if his favorite piece, "Gao Shan Liu Shui"— *high mountains and running waters*, was in it.

He loved *Zheng* music and often attended public performances, but he had never seen a real *Zheng* so close before. The beauty of the ancient instrument grabbed him. He felt a temptation to pluck a string with his own finger and hear the lingering sound clouting the hollow wood, but he controlled himself.

"Is it too late to go there?" he asked.

". . . No. I'll see if I can get permission for a couple of days off."

It took him a while to make sense of the notion that she needed permission.

4.

Although it was already mid-autumn, the Balang Mountains were still astonishingly beautiful. The group of twenty-some adventure lovers stayed overnight in the Wolong panda preservation zone, and climbed on a truck to go up into the uninhabited mountains the next morning. No tourist buses went this way; but they managed to find a truck driver who did not mind using his state-owned company's vehicle to make some money on the side.

The mountain road was narrow and bumpy. The passengers standing and swaying on the open truck had to hold on to the sides tightly. But soon the girls' nervous facial expressions turned to amazement. Now and then milky fogs drifted off the steep cliff on the roadside, slowly diffusing above them. On the hills light-green woods layered with dark-green woods. Time to time a burning-red wild cherry unexpectedly appeared. Most of the wild flowers had withered between clumps of bushes, adding a bit of solemnity to the autumn atmosphere; but yellow Pony Foots, red Honey Flowers, and purple Bear Beads had just started blooming. In a stop requested by the girls who wanted to take pictures, the driver said they were a few days too late to see the peak, when the blossoms on the hills could stop a jaded driver who had run this road for a quarter-century.

The group got off the truck halfway to one of the peaks. As soon as their hiking started, Shiao Su played the pleasant cavalier for his female classmates. He carried one's bag and another's wild bouquet. He cut a tree branch for a girl to use as a cane, and he brought up the rear to make sure no one strayed.

Qian-qian did not come. "Too many people," she had mumbled.

Shiao Su subconsciously looked for the scene in Dandelion's painting, but he could not decide if he had found it. They were alike and not alike. Despite his indecisive observations, he experienced an unfamiliar sense of peacefulness. This sense diluted his regrets that Qian-qian had not wanted to come. Still, he had hoped to rediscover that strong feeling that had so startled him when he first saw Dandelion's painting. Why did it not come? Was this the distinction between reality and arts? He did not know.

He looked around for Yue Zhu, but she had gone too far ahead.

He had heard that Yue Zhu got along with the women students well last night; she'd even drawn a sketch for each of the girls. "Looked like the real me!" a woman classmate had told Shiao Su early in the morning when they were looking for the missing Yue Zhu. She appeared just before the truck started, morning dew on her hair and grass tips on her skirt. In her hand was a sketchbook. After they got off the truck, she quickly walked ahead of everyone, her green ribbon hidden, then showing, hidden, then showing between trees. Several times the desire to catch up with her caught Shiao Su, but he controlled the impulse, aware of the classmates around him.

He lost his chance again when the group stopped at the viewpoint "sea of clouds," as Yue Zhu named it. This was a mountain mouth where the waves of clouds rolled under everyone's feet. Girls screamed and boys whistled with happy astonishment, while Yue Zhu patiently waited for them. "*Water is hardly water after seeing the oceans / Clouds are no longer clouds apart from Wu Mountains,*" the ancient poem flared in Shiao Su's mind. How many mountains had she trudged alone? Had she also been in the mysterious Wu Mountains? He hesitated, wanting to go talk to her. Before he could decide she had turned to continue leading the way up, leaving him behind again.

They climbed till they reached a small woods near the peak where, the girls exhausted, the group stopped for a long lunch break. Shiao Su noticed that Yue Zhu had disappeared again. He sat under a pine tree and thought for a while. He looked around to see if anyone was watching. Then he stood up and went to search in the woods.

He strolled along a path winding upward in fog. The fog was getting thicker. In a short time the fog wrapped him tightly, pushing an icy coldness into his skin and bones. He began to feel impatient. Where did Yue Zhu go? He trotted for a while, making loud whistles, but could hear nothing other than the wind's garrulousness. Not even the birds were making noise. He walked, then trotted again as the fog began to thin. The fog was gradually disappearing. Suddenly, before he was aware, his whole body was showered in vast dazzling sunshine.

He had reached the top, the highest point in the Balang Mountains, almost to the snow line. What emerged in front of his eyes was an incredible picture. On one side of the mountain dark-gray fogs thickly wrapped secluded forests; on the other side bright sunlight shone on the green pines. The sunny side of the mountain presented layers and layers of colors, their contours distinct and powerful. In the remote yet clear distance, the Four Girls Mountains, perennially covered with snow, stood tall and erect, the whiteness blinding. He was transfixed. For the first time in the hiking, an unnamed emotion arose.

He was unaware of how long he had been standing when he heard a faint sound from afar. He pricked up his ears, only to find a vast quietness. He walked in the direction the sound had come from and searched. Gradually the sound became more audible. It was a person's voice. He ran forward. Then he stopped.

Not too far from him, Yue Zhu stood on a black rock, letting herself go and reading aloud along the wind. There was a wildness in her hoarse voice:

> "…Go collide savage wind
> Taste freedom's conception
> Go shower brilliant sunlight
> Experience the ungrudging forest
> Go dive like fearless water
> Or circle around in the abyss
> Go to the funeral for withered vines
> Sing for the moss and pray for lone cliff
> Go scream in total strangeness
> Complete all your impulses
> Go feel yourself eternal
> Renew your soul with bare passion…"

Mountain winds blew the words far away; indistinct echoes fell among the hills. He had not written these words as beautifully as he heard them now. When silence returned to the mountains, Shiao Su found himself frozen, his chest congested. Except the girl who wore a green ribbon flowing with her waterfall black hair, nothing seemed real. Another blast of wind blew over and awakened him. He quickly turned and ran away as fast as he could.

That evening they came down the mountains too late and had to stay in a small hotel on the road. The exhausted group got into their beds with no time to mind the hotel's unclean and crude condition. Shiao Su lay under the cold, hard quilt and listened to the strange sound of the night outside for a long, long time.

5.

During the next few weeks Shiao Su visited the art gallery a few more times. If there was any change in the gallery, it was almost imperceptible. Yet he went there again and again, unaware what he was looking for.

He told his parents and Qian-qian that he was too busy studying and changed his practice of returning home from every week to every other week. His grades in every subject went down. He appeared in the track fields less and less frequently and smoked more and more cigarettes.

He did not know what he was waiting for. It was not a call because there was only one phone in the entire dormitory building, which was in the janitor's room downstairs. He was not waiting for a letter either; he got more letters than others, but he knew without looking that none were that important. Still, he waited.

On a Saturday evening when Shiao Su had not gone home for the second week in a row, Qian-qian rode her bike to campus to look for him. She asked for directions several times to find his dorm, only to see most windows in the building were dark. It was a clear evening with a sky full of stars, and a Saturday movie was playing in the big field outside the men's dorms. Qian-qian almost wept: how could she find Shiao Su in the dark crowds?

She walked up to room 201 in desperation, and was surprised to see the door was ajar. A ray of dim light leaked out the crack. All the happiness of life returned to her heart and she quickly knocked on the door. When she did not hear an answer, she gave a little push to the door. Under a table lamp, she saw Shiao Su was alone, asleep on his arms, a book thicker than a brick opened in front of him. Beside the book, cigarette stubs filled an ashtray. She walked to him tip-toe and gently shook his shoulder.

Shiao Su opened his sleepy eyes and was confused for a few seconds.

"How . . . how come you are here?"

"I want you to come home with me."

He did not know what to say so he said he needed to go to the bathroom. When he went, Qian-qian sat down and waited. To pass the time she read the open page, page 3484, of the big book in front of her:

Entry: "Gao Shan Liu Shui"
Source: *Liezi,* "Tang Wen"
Period: Han Dynasty
   Boya excelled at playing Zheng, Ziqi personified listening.
Boya's music craving for mountains, Ziqi exclaimed, "towering
high cliffs." Boya's music admiring rivers, Ziqi proclaimed,
"gracious running waters." Ziqi died, Boya smashed the Zheng
and never played again.

The text was in archaic Chinese. Qian-qian did not recognize several words and she could not understand the context. This was not like a textbook of any of Shiao Su's subjects. In fact she had never seen Shiao Su bring this book home before.

Shiao Su came back and saw Qian-qian's questioning expression. He closed the big book and said to her, "Let's go home."

Sunday they went to the West Suburb Bridge farmers' market together. While Qian-qian bargained with the farmers, Shiao Su walked to the art gallery. He hesitated at the door but eventually stepped in.

And he saw it at once. The painting "Balang Mountains" was gone. In its place was a new black-and-white woodcut print titled "No Subject" by Dandelion. On the picture were barren hills populated by only two young willow trees, their long thin branches whipping in wind. The appearance of the picture was so simple it was more like a photo. Under the picture frame was a poem by Ai Qing, an old-generation poet from before the Cultural Revolution:

One tree, another
Stand in separation
Wind and air
Telling their distance
Below the soil
Their roots extend
In invisible depth
They entangle together

It finally came. The message he had been waiting for.

After weeks of internal storms, this message was more a verification than a shock. For the first time he clearly saw that an other-worldly life could become reality. A moist green meadow studded with tiny yellow flowers. A flock of sheep grazing lazily on the meadow. A little log house in the woods. A *Zheng* and a steaming teapot in the house. A long trudge no longer lonely. An understanding without words . . .

He did not hear the footsteps but a familiar, intimate scent pulled him back to the present world. He half-turned and saw Qian-qian's innocent eyes. For a second he thought he detected a thread of fear in her dark brown pupils, pupils that reminded him of a little deer who sensed a hidden prayer.

"What do you see?" Shiao Su asked softly.

"Pictures and a poem." Qian-qian pointed to the wall with her free hand.

"What else do you see?"

"Just artworks. Aren't they? Just artworks. Nothing real," she said a little too quickly.

Shiao Su did not say anything more. He took the full hand-basket from her without putting an arm around her shoulder. They walked out of the gallery in silence. Outside the gallery, under the autumn sun, farmers hawking their wares not too far away were clearly discernible.

That evening Qian-qian cried very hard over a trivial issue. She shed tears like rain and there was only one promise that could console her. When she finally fell asleep with tears still glistening in the corners of her eyes, Shiao Su wrote a new poem. At the end of it were the following lines:

> *Only now I know*
> *I can't be enlarged*
> *Nor yet shrunk.*
> *— Is it too late?*

6.

In late fall, the changing political winds carried an overdue tenseness to the distant Sichuan basin. China's new leadership had demolished the "Democracy Wall" in Beijing and arrested activists who posted opinions and poetry on that wall. The same activists had earlier risked their lives pushing the current leadership into power. Little was novel in this game; in the many thousands of years of China's history, the emperor in every dynasty had killed the donkey the moment it left the millstone.

If Shiao Su was disappointed at the news that his friends failed to obtain an imprimatur for printing his work, he did not show it. He mounted his bike and rode off campus without delay. Yue Zhu needed to be informed as soon as possible; all the typesetting and printing activities must be stopped. If the authorities found out about an unapproved printing she, and everyone involved, could be arrested.

It was another dusk and the setting sun was little by little slanting into rosy clouds. There was a filament of coldness in the autumn air. Shiao Su's bike crunched the fallen leaves across half of the city. At the printing shop he stood his bike against the wall, not taking the time to lock it, and hurriedly walked on to the hallway that led to Yue Zhu's room.

The sound of a familiar piece of *Zheng* music slowed down his steps. His heart pictured Yue Zhu's lean fingers stroking the long strings. Wood hammering metal, breakers dashing on rocks, waters falling off the cliff, echoes fading in the valley . . . for how many thousands of years had this soul-searching "Gao Shan Liu Shui" been played and listened to? Shiao Su leaned his forehead against the closed door and shut his eyes. The vibration of the *Zheng* strings passed through the door to his body. He lost the courage to knock on the door.

Peng! A sudden sound, the sound of a taut metal string snapping, sprung Shiao Shu's forehead off the door. He heard her wince inside. He stepped back in panic. This could not be happening! This should only be in folklore! That an instrument's string would break if someone who truly understood the music were eavesdropping . . .

The door opened. Yue Zhu smiled at him; he could see the pleasure brought by his unexpected visit. He quickly adjusted himself and said "hi" to her. He went in with her and sat down by her square tea table. When she was pouring tea for him he saw the fresh red line across the back of her left hand. His throat tightened.

He sipped tea and searched for words. He could not find any.

"I wrote one for you," he finally said. A thin layer of scarlet flushed over her cheeks, then quickly faded. "Could I please read it to you?"

"Yes."

He started to read the poem; his voice flat and dry.

> "*Snow Line*
>
> *Far, far away*
> *Dandelion*

Absorb the sun's melody

This shore, the other one
Two light spots
One became the moon
One became the sun

Let's play blocks
You and me
Use these odds and ends
Form an entirely new continent
We will smile
Then push them down

A great skeleton
Near the snow line
Silent

My sketch was lost
The lines of flowing water
Graceful green silk
All gone, to the woods of another mountain

The earth forever quiet
Only the uninhabited South Pole
Aurora and meteors
Use the same language to love

I walk to the end of the valley
Winds blow to the universe
Can life return to folktale?

Farewell, birch forest . . ."

Yue Zhu's head lowered in the middle of his reading. Her two hands held the teacup with no movement. When he finished, he did not dare to look at her. He stared at his own teacup, weak steam still wafting up.

"This is the last poem I'll ever write," he said after a while, still not looking at her. The light tone denied the weight of his decision. He did not expect a reply. He thought he could melt in this endless silence, right here, in this cozy little room, and that could actually make him very happy. Then he heard an almost inaudible laughter from Yue Zhu.

He had never known laughter could rend his heart harder than tears. He reached for her hand on the table, his palm covering its fresh bruise. For the first time since he arrived, he looked into her eyes. The eyes were an autumn lake with thousands of ripples. The bare pain in his gaze burned down the dam of the lake; it could no longer hold the water . . .

* * *

Twenty years later, an authoritative expert on literary history, who had entered a different university the same year as Shiao Su, published a three-volume monograph on western China's poetry. He wrote:

"In the early 1980s, the first and by far most outstanding lyric poet in western China was Shiao Su. On many campuses I heard students reciting his poems. To this day it is still a mystery why he suddenly gave up writing. With his talent, he could have become one of the greatest poets in contemporary China.

"I visited Shiao Su and his wife several years after he put down his pen for good. He had become a top manager of a state enterprise. But he was not happy."

The monograph included the entire poem of "Golden Bell," with no trace of "Snow Line." It did not mention anything about Yue Zhu. The author of the monograph may or may not have known Yue Zhu, but his book wasn't about arts, let alone religious arts. Yue Zhu, in fact, later became a Buddhist artist after she met a hundred-year-old priest in a Buddhist temple on E'mei Mountain. The priest said to her, "Nothingness is possession, possession is nothingness." She became the priest's "closing-gate disciple" — his last student. After the priest's parinirvana, some had seen Yue Zhu traveling alone between Buddhist mountains. If you visit Buddhist temples in Sichuan's mountains today, chances are you will come across her wall-size paintings. #

PIVOT POINT

1.

The first time Lanbo asked me to wait for him, it was Su Ting's poem that flashed through my mind: "Wait for love to walk into the sun." I want to travel with you to every mountain, every water, I told him, and he said, when the time comes, *any* place is a good place.

Let's wait for a pivot point, he said. He looked as determined to survive divorce as Rambo was to survive war. "Lanbo" was the Chinese pronunciation of "Rambo." Our mutual friend Old Brother gave him this nickname when American movies gushed through the newly opened gate of China, together with Rambo-style jackets and sand-washed Lee jeans.

Meanwhile, ashamed of a daughter yet to be betrothed at age 26, my mother begged all her acquaintances to match-make for me. I saw in her eyes the fear that I would soon be joining the large crowd of "aging youth," a peculiar 1980s label for leftover urban women unable to find mates. During the Cultural Revolution, an entire generation had been sent to the countryside, and spent the best part of their youth in alien fields, determined not to marry until allowed back to the city. When they did finally return, the men went for younger girls, while their female peers were left to age alone. It was like the aftermath of war, except that the men were wed instead of dead.

But I never considered myself one of those women — after all, I had been in the countryside for only a couple of years, having been caught in the epilogue of that movement.

As a result of my mother's exertions, it was not uncommon for a stranger (usually with a college degree) to intrude upon my weekend solitude. So on a Sunday morning, when an immaculately dressed young man arrived with an old man, I dutifully pulled out chairs and offered them tea in the living room, then politely excused myself and retreated to my bedroom. But the young man followed me and held open my door as I tried to shut it. "I came to see you, not your parents," he said, clamping on. His boldness raised my curiosity. "What for?" I asked. He glanced at the book in my hand — the Chinese translation of Prigogine's *Exploring Complexity*, and said, "I've long heard of your overflowing brilliance. I would like to have a chat with you."

Fine then. I liked challenges from men. Our chat started easily but soon our lips became spears and our tongues turned to swords. We argued over whether Prigogine the Nobel laureate's new theory settled the famous debate between Einstein and Bohr — about whether God played dice with the universe. When the young man left with his uncle a few hours later, he looked impressed and I'd had good fun.

I did not expect to hear from this man again, so when his remarks filtered back through his uncle to my mother and then to me, I was not at all pleased: "She is too high to reach." Of course we all knew too well this unwritten Chinese convention, implying that I was a woman not worth dating. After all, "No talent is the virtue of a woman," Confucius had said thousands of years ago, and no one had forgotten it since.

I was not as smart when I felt insulted. I looked up the address of his institute in the phonebook, walked to a pay phone on the street below his office building, and dialed his number. Since he had come to chat with me out of curiosity the first time, I presumed he would come to meet me this time as well. And he did come, but hardly looking as relaxed as when we'd first met. We stood on the sidewalk staring at each other, a bus passing by and bureaucratically throwing dirt on us. "What is it?" he asked. "What on earth makes you look down at me?" I snapped back. That, producing the opposite of my intended effect, cleared up his puzzlement as if I had just granted him an advantage. "I am honestly looking up at you," he replied in an innocent and matter-of-fact manner, "but wouldn't it be too tiring to look up to my wife everyday?" The frankness in his answer muted me. What was I doing? Begging to be his wife? Or begging him to understand a different kind of woman? Either way I was doomed to fail. In shame I turned and left. "You'll make a worthy friend, though," he said to my back.

At home, I looked around my simple bedroom for anything feminine—

white bedspread, black-white checkered quilt, a gray calligraphy penholder and an untidy pile of books on a worn, nut-brown desk. There was no hint of gender anywhere. I sat dazed on the edge of my bed. This was the ironic side of being an educated Chinese woman. Your learnedness scared men away. They just wanted their women cute, obedient, and good at posing.

Fortunately — or unfortunately — Lanbo was not one of them. "I've never met a woman as real as you are," he said, fixing a long look at me until I turned away with embarrassment. "Can't say you are really pretty," he added, "but you surely warrant a long look."

2.

My mother chose not to acknowledge that one hand can't clap. When she began to view every bachelor as a suitable son-in-law, I finally had to tell her I would rather be in love with a man I couldn't marry than marry a man I didn't love. As if I had a choice.

My sensitive mother was at once alarmed. She asked me if there in fact was such a man; if so what man was he, a worker or a cadre? In Western terms this was equivalent to asking "Blue collar or white collar?" Until she asked, the question had never entered my mind. It wasn't his fault that he did not have a middle-school diploma — no one in his generation did. It was the Cultural Revolution for Mao's sake! Despite my college education, he had read many more prohibited books than I, including the black market translation of *Lady Chatterley's Lover*. Once, before we became lovers, I visited the warehouse where he worked and found his boss requesting that he attend an "anti-illiteracy" class. He and I made fun of that episode nonstop until it got boring.

I was afraid my mother's next question would be why I loved him. What could I tell her? That he could mimic Rambo as vividly as he emulated Chairman Mao and made me laugh? That I enjoyed his coarse palm stroking my bare skin in the dark?

But my mother had already wrapped her fist around the core: he was a married man. She did not say much, for which I considered myself lucky. Who'd have expected her stern face when he greeted her on his first visit! Lanbo was so embarrassed that he lost all his wit; he lowered his head and left. I wept bitterly and refused to talk to my mother for weeks, thinking a thousand times about leaving home, but having nowhere to go. Houses were owned and assigned by the government, and for many years there had been no extra houses to assign to anyone. In the city it was not unusual for a young married couple to share a single room with their parents, each listening to every squeak from the other bed. I was the envy of many because I had my own bedroom in my parents' house.

Thus I stayed, just not talking to my mother, while she, unable to bear my silence, cooked my favorite dishes — her way of making peace with me.

And Lanbo came again. There was no other safe place for us: the eyes of China's masses were nets above and snares below. He knocked on the front door, not greeting whoever opened it, and kept his eyes to the floor as he sliced through the thistles and thorns of my family's gazes. As soon as he stepped into my bedroom, he deadbolted the door. When his generous warm lips touched mine I forgot all else. Tips of two tongues twirling and thrusting, we sucked each other out of breath, letting go to take air then tightly wrapping onto each other again. We could never have enough, as if our tongues were doing the lovemaking that our bodies were not permitted.

3.

I went to see Old Brother, one of the few friends who knew about our predicament. It was in his house that I had first met Lanbo. But I could not bring myself to say anything. How could I speak such unspeakable things to a man friend?

You are being serious again, Old Brother said, I told you not to be so serious. You won't be suffering if you are not serious. No matter how serious you are, it is nothing but an affair, a scandal.

But it is love, I mumbled.

No, it's sexual desire, Old Brother said. Grow up, little girl. Where is your intelligence when it comes to these matters?

I will prove to you it's love, I thought. But I didn't say it. Instead came these words: Why can't he divorce?

Old Brother sighed. It's not that he doesn't want a divorce. He can't. Going through the divorce process is like peeling a man's skin alive. Look around — any woman who wants a divorce can get one. Have you ever heard of a man succeeding if he wants a divorce? You think he likes to go home? After years of marriage, men have not even a tiny bit of desire left toward their wives. All are like this.

I didn't like the word "desire"; it had a filthy sound that blasphemed love. I gaped at Old Brother, my fool's mouth hanging open. After a while I asked if what he said was true. Yes, all husbands are like this, Old Brother confirmed. Then he added in a teasing — or perhaps truthful — tone, "It could've been me instead of him."

I walked slowly out of Old Brother's house and did not go home right away. Instead, I took the stone path down hundreds of steps to the river. On the rocky beach where Lanbo and I once sat snuggling in the dark, I sauntered back and forth. What did *she* look like? How did she feel? From Lanbo's occasional words about her, she must have been a kind and obedient wife. She was a mother who loved her son more than her own life. Sometimes, with a long sigh, Lanbo would wish she were a shrew. If so, things for us would be easier, he'd said.

Perhaps she sensed something but kept silent, as a wise wife would. Perhaps she convinced herself not to believe the rumors. She could endure anything to keep her husband and her family, just as I endured the pain of our love. It is not without reason that the Chinese character for "endure" is a knife atop a heart.

At the gate of my parents' apartment building, a figure stood in the shadows.

"I have waited for two hours," he said hoarsely.

I wanted to collapse into his arms, but I had to restrain myself. There were eyes peering from at least one window. Together we walked up the stairs and passed through the gloomy gazes of my parents. As I closed my bedroom door behind us, my father loudly scolded my younger sister. *You should have morals! You should know shame!* I turned my stereo to the highest volume, but Lanbo turned it back to normal.

He sat there, stupefied. I don't demand a divorce, I said, putting a smile on my face. I want only your love. Marriage is just paper, I don't care. Look at the bright side — we have every weekday evening together.

I felt relieved, even a bit noble.

He grabbed me and held me so tight that I lost my breath. When he finally looked up, his eyes were glistening with tears. Then his hoarse voice again:

"I must marry you in this life!"

4.

When life began again in spring, he didn't go home one Sunday. We climbed up a wild hill in the Southern Mountains and sat in the meadow. The blinding sunshine in this uninhabited place pleased Lanbo so much that he lay facing the sky, four limbs spread on the grass. Eyes closed, he told his "insert" stories: walking days and nights along a river to fish; lying naked on the beach under the sun. His voice intimate, warm, and far, as if in a dream. I took out an issue of *World Science* from my bag - there was no more perfect moment to read.

Just when I turned the page to an interesting article, he knocked the magazine out of my hands, pulled me down on the grass, and yelled with joy, "Damn you reading at such a moment!" So we lay shoulder to shoulder on the grass and narrowed our eyes to squint at the blue sky, white clouds, and the golden sun spotting through the leaves of a big banyan tree. He asked what I was reading. Karl Popper, I said. What did that foreigner have to say? Oh why don't you read it too, I sat up and tried to reach the magazine. He pinned my arm down. I want you to tell me, he said. Okay, the old man said science is not truth, rather it's the ever changing conjecture of human rationality. Science advances by deductive *falsification* instead of verification. He turned and eyed me for a moment. So, he said, what we learned in school is all wrong? Our way of thinking is all wrong? I was surprised by his question and gave it careful thought. He was right — Popper's theory was indeed different from the historical materialism taught. How come I felt Popper to be so naturally logical and did not even notice its anti-materialism?

Who cares about Popper or Pepper, he laughed, I'll just think the way I do. Does philosophy serve any damn purpose? I'm better off without it! You're sexier without it! Then with the suddenness of a thunderbolt, he sat up and kicked the magazine, which made several somersaults rolling down the hill. I widened my eyes and watched helplessly as it disappeared from sight. "It's especially annoying when a woman talks philosophy!" he added. I was upset at first, then all of a sudden felt ashamed at the redundancy of thought.

He placed his wide callused palm on my breast. The hand paused, then tightened its grip. He glanced to the left, the right, the rear, then began to unbuckle my jeans. I closed my eyes. Tree leaves prattled garrulously, and a cool breeze gently stroked my belly.

Flap! A sound, heavy as a rock falling, shook my eyes open. Lanbo was gazing at something above, his face blanched, his fingers frozen on his zipper.

I propped my head up and turned to see a pair of big dirty bare feet on the grass.

"I am People's Militia!" the dark-faced peasant announced, imposing his rifle on Lanbo. "Get up, go with me to the Commune!"

Lanbo got up with effort, his pant legs trembling in the wind. He said, "Listen, brother, I didn't do anything."

"Shut up, rapist! I have been watching you from up in the tree for quite a while!"

But you jumped down a little too soon, I thought.

"He's not a rapist," I said. "He's my boyfriend." The word "boyfriend" came from my lips with euphoria. I had never had a chance to use it before.

The peasant blinked, apparently baffled by my ingratitude, and he refused to address me. He shouted at Lanbo: "Then you are a thug! No good man will do this thing in the wild. Move, go with me now!"

Lanbo fished a bill out of his pant pocket. "Brother, get some cigarettes for yourself."

"Don't insult me with your stinky money!" A slap hit Lanbo's face with a crisp sound. I waited for Lanbo to strike back; instead he cupped his cheek. "I'll go with you, but you let her go." His voice came out with muffled heroism as he leered at the rifle's black muzzle. He must have been picturing the torture and humiliation ahead, and himself holding my name unto his death.

"He's my boyfriend! Are you deaf? He's not a thug! I'm a government researcher!" I jumped up and yelled at the peasant. I took out my red work ID and pushed it into his face. "Can you see? Can you see? You insult and beat a government cadre! You are the thug!"

The peasant stared at me at a loss. I dragged Lanbo's hand and said, "Let's go! Who wants to talk to a thug!"

We sauntered away as casually as possible. After a hundred meters I looked back, the peasant still standing there watching us. As soon as we got out of his sight, though, Lanbo pulled his hand from mine. "Don't let others see us like this," he said.

He did not visit me for several days after that. When he showed up again neither of us mentioned the incident.

5.

Now we spent all our time within walls. Each weeknight between 7 and 10, Lanbo and I rendezvoused behind my bedroom door. Then he went back to sleep alone in his shabby dorm next to his warehouse while I tossed and turned in my queen bed longing for him. Each Saturday he took the long-distance bus back to his wife and son in a northern suburb, returning to work on Monday morning. We hadn't had a night together since he broke my hymen over a year ago in a friend's home, and our welcome there was long worn out. We couldn't check into a hotel either - a marriage certificate and matching photo IDs were required.

So, more than anything else I wanted to have my own apartment. And as the Economic Reform unfolded, this goal — once unreachable — came within my grasp.

I worked for the Economics Research Center of the government, where I was building a comprehensive simulation model for our city's development. Recently, for the first time in decades, our work unit had constructed a new apartment building for employees. When the assignment process for the new apartments began, a war also began. Each day a surfeit of people in their early 20s to late 40s descended on the housing office, and I found myself among them, abandoning my usual disdain for crowds.

A woman who processed data in my office was always ahead of me in line. A couple of years older and with more seniority, she too was single. "Horse face," she was nicknamed because of her long chin. Only by smiling could she shorten her face into something close to normal, so she smiled a lot. In the housing office, though, she quarreled and begged loudly and nonstop, her chin longer than ever. When she didn't get anywhere, she would look around to vent her frustration. This behavior became so predictable that I always managed to escape before her vulgar remarks fell on me, but a new colleague was less lucky. He had recently graduated from college, too new to have any hope for an apartment; I suspected he was only there to gain experiences for a future housing war. Horse Face jeered at him, practically neighing, and called him a "warty toad lusting after a swan's flesh."

After failed efforts to settle numerous fights, the authorities decided to score employees not by their age but by total working years plus marital status. Fortunately, the time I had spent as an insert in the countryside and as a student at the university counted, giving me six additional years, and putting me last on the list of lucky employees, the only one unmarried. Horse Face did not get in. It turned out that years ago she had avoided the countryside with a fake diagnosis of some strange disease, making her total working years fewer than mine. I was so thrilled at the thought of my own apartment that I woke up in the night giggling.

I told Lanbo the good news. He was skeptical. Happiness comes alone while misfortune loves company, he said, citing an adage. His words made me check back over years of my life, and I felt a bit easier when I found nothing that could be called happiness.

I went to the housing office as soon as they issued keys.

"You are not on the list," the clerk said as he checked for my name.

"I *am*. The last one." I smiled.

He looked again carefully and shook his head. He showed me the list. In place of my name was that of Horse Face.

"But her score was lower than mine!" I cried.

The man patiently took more papers from his drawer. Before he finished checking the scores, to my astonishment, two people walked in hand-in-hand: Horse Face dressed in bright pink, and Warty Toad in a western suit. Horse Face grinned like a blooming flower as she generously stuffed a handful of Double Happiness candies in my pocket.

It turned out that the two had gotten their marriage certificate the day before, raising Horse Face's score above mine.

On their moving day, I stood in a far corner outside the new building, watching Horse Face and Warty Toad quarrelling and transporting furniture to the apartment that would have belonged to me, daydreaming the freedom that my own space would have brought, while silently cursing their dirty strategy. It would be too late when they found out how difficult it was to get rid of a marriage certificate, and that would be their punishment.

I angrily added a housing parameter to my simulation model. If I'd been alone, I would have chewed and swallowed the bitterness myself, then forgotten about it. Now I turned to Lanbo for consolation, calling and asking to meet him at my home right away. I had never before asked to see him during the workday. He slipped out of his warehouse and came to me. What happened? he asked. Nothing, I said, but could we have a night together? How about tonight? We haven't been together for a long time, have we? My voice shivered.

I want to be with you too, he said, and held my face in his palms; but we have no place. You know we have no place to go.

Could you please find a place? Please?

He sat down and his head slumped. You know I can't find one, he said.

We can never have unrestrained sex in China.

My tears came without warning. I cried so hard that the sky darkened and the floor sank. He sat with no words for me. When I had cried myself out, he told me to take care, and went back to work.

6.

Then came a *pivot point*.

My parents, who were always traveling on business when I was little but never again after I grew up, went to visit my older sister, who lived with her husband in a neighboring city. That gave us three full days. Lanbo and I took sick leave from work, and we brought in plenty of food so we wouldn't need to set foot outside. We planned to ignore any knocks on the door.

The first night it took him several hours to overcome his humiliation before he could undress in my parents' house. Faint sounds next door and footsteps upstairs alarmed him even though the door was bolted from the inside. All the while remaining dressed, he held my nude body tightly in his arms. Vast heat from his chest penetrated his clothes and enveloped me, his prickly chin pressing against my soft cheek. His palms roamed my body, sometimes gentle, sometimes uneasy, until his strokes lulled me to sleep. I curled like a kitten against his broad chest. In the middle of the night he attacked me with colossal emotion. Half asleep, half awake, I lifted my face to the almost unbearable pleasure. Even with my eyes closed in the darkness I could feel his, bright and shining. His male softness and rudeness poised in the rise and fall of his body. I told him I wanted to die at that moment; in such pleasure, death did not seem frightening. Don't be silly, he said, smiling. I murmured, then let us do it all night, and he laughed quietly.

The next day we stayed in bed except to fill our empty stomachs and to go to the bathroom. The second night was as joyful, and smoother, but hard knocks on the door early in the morning scared us witless. We were frozen until I recognized Old Brother's voice and reluctantly opened the door. He walked to Lanbo and said venomously, "You really are here! I've looked for you everywhere! Your wife is in the hospital! In critical condition!" He threw these words at Lanbo without looking at me, as if to avoid something.

Lanbo quickly dressed and left with Old Brother, saying little, shooting me a glance I could not decipher.

He disappeared for two weeks. When he was not with me I thought a lot — mostly about whether his wife would be all right or not, or rather, whether she might die. I could hardly tell if I was hoping for or afraid of her death. It was a very long two weeks.

When he finally showed up again, he said simply, "She's better now." He told me she had appendicitis, though I hadn't asked. Then he sat numb like a wooden log, no words and no movement, for some while.

"Do you want me to tell you the truth?" He lifted his eyes, stared at me, and, not waiting for my answer, said, "I must tell you…Who else can I tell otherwise? I must tell you this…"

Then he said:

"There was a moment, by her hospital bed, I wished her to die . . . but only for a few seconds, I swear . . ." He grabbed his hair with one hand, crying out lowly like a wolf:

"My heavens, what man have I become?"

His words emptied a bottle of five spices in my stomach. I did not know what woman I had become either. I did not know what was changing us.

That was how the pivot point passed. Life went on as usual after that: he still spent every weekday evening with me and went home every weekend.

And I gloomily added another parameter, the stableness of family, to my model.

7.

A philosopher friend came to say goodbye to me after being accepted by a small university in the U.S. to study for his Ph.D. He was the one who'd once asked my motivation for living. His was responsibility, he said, and I said mine was curiosity. Paradox! He'd warned, using a word that we mathematicians try hard to avoid. You are longing for tomorrow, but you should be rejecting tomorrow. You say you want to live and yet you are looking to death? Doesn't tomorrow mean one day closer to death?

During his visit he told me a true story that went like this:

A man stood managing his breathing in the exercise of *qi gong*. In the half-ring of spectators surrounding him were white-bearded scholars, government officials, newspaper reporters, authoritative experts, and skeptical scientists.

Not far from the man was a solid brick wall.

The man started to walk toward it. Unblinking gazes followed his steps. He walked forward slowly and continued through the bricks.

"What did you feel when you went through?" an expert asked. The man said he saw tiny cracks that expanded wide enough to let him in.

My philosopher friend was a steady, taciturn scholar. He was there in the half-ring of spectators. I asked him if he really believed what he saw — an apparently redundant question.

He explained that in the "super-functional" man's space — a space overlapped with ours, the man's thoughts controlled material; in our space it was the opposite. "Our mind is the prisoner of our body," he said in his deep voice.

Later I would be bewitched reading a story about Wittgenstein. The world-famous philosopher once asked his students, "What would we say if I walk through this wall?" The students thought he was really going to do it, but of course he didn't. He couldn't. The question I had was, did my philosopher friend know this story about Wittgenstein before he witnessed a man going through a wall? If so, did Wittgenstein's words affect his belief in what he saw at a subconscious level?

I told Lanbo the story about the super-functional man, careful not to use any philosophical terms. He said, "Nonsense. Walls just can't be walked through."

It was that simple and factual.

What was I in? A crisis that was neither war nor earthquake but an impasse where all was well and nothing could be done?

8.

So we waited for another pivot point. Each evening we met, we kissed, we quarreled, we chatted, we cried, like a true couple, except for the one thing that couples do. Yet I was so accustomed to his presence in my life that if he did not show up in the evening, I could not get any work done the whole next day.

I waited with him from winter to spring, from spring to summer. Winter had long gone, spring no longer returned, fall was here again; still he had not said anything to his wife.

One night in my bedroom we watched a movie on TV about a man living with a wife and four concubines in the 1920s. Lanbo commented with envy, "What a comfortable life!" "Not to me," I said. He quickly changed the topic, and that raised my suspicion.

I designed a simple psychological test in my mind, then tried it on him.

"If the two of us run into a natural disaster on a mountain, like an avalanche or mudslide, what would you think first?"

"That won't happen."

"What if it does?"

"Run. One gets away, good. Two get away, better," he said with no hesitation, then asked me with alarm, "What would you do?"

"I want to be with you, alive or dead."

"Woman," he said.

"I am a supplement in your spare time, right?"

He didn't answer. Storm clouds accumulated on his face while I asked again, spellbound.

"Ask such annoying things and you want me to come again?" he said, and took to his heels. His hand stopped on the doorknob. Then he turned to face me. "Am I really as bad as you thought?"

"Let's run away," I begged.

"Are you being impractical again?" he asked. "Where can we run? Besides, I don't want to run. We can only wait, let time arrange everything."

I took a long shower after he left, examining myself closely for the first time. I carefully massaged every part of my body, knowing it was as graceful and beautiful as ever. The body was still young; getting old was my heart. At this moment I felt — not just thought — that human life is such a rare thing, a treasure. But only if I could spend it in a style of my own choosing could I say I was treasuring it. I saw such a lifestyle like the horizon — the harder I walked toward it, the further it receded.

The latest parameter I added was for lifestyle choice.

9.

As colorful lines folded and unfolded on my computer screen, forming grotesque shapes, my tapping on the keyboard became nervous and errors occurred more frequently. My heart pounded in anticipation. Following my clicks, the curves changed; regular oscillations gradually became irregular and unpredictable. At last, the entire screen was a fantastic, unrecognizable chaos.

Success!

I found several parameters whose smallest changes were magnified by the system to the extent that chaos ensued. My model revealed the stochastic nature of a social economic system, as well as its causes. For the first time in China, human behavioral factors were introduced into an economic model. A myriad of choices, the number of people making choices, and the coordination of these choices eventually led to the system's high unpredictability.

To my surprise, my simulation model was admired and loudly praised even before its official review. What's more, a few reformists in the city government who advocated complete open-market economy regarded my model as scientific proof of their opinions, which showed how much the politicians knew about science. The mayor, a relatively young reformist leader in his early fifties, even received me in his office and promised to help me obtain a significant scientific award. He asked my age, which reminded me I was one day short of thirty. Good, good, the mayor said, the age of standing. His juggling of allusion did not impress me. Everyone knew the saying from Confucius: "Standing at thirty, unconfused at forty, knowing destiny at fifty."

"Young intellectuals are our Party's treasure; we must take care of them well." After giving instructions to his male secretary, who faithfully nodded while taking down his boss's words, the mayor turned to ask if I had any personal requests.

I said I wished that unmarried and married women had equal rights to an apartment.

"You don't have an apartment?" The mayor looked surprised. "My apologies," he said seriously. "An outstanding comrade like you deserves special consideration. We will resolve the issue for you. Believe in the Party!"

I felt more detached than I would have expected. It was Saturday morning. Lanbo wouldn't come to me today.

I returned home to find a letter from my philosopher friend, urging me to go west. *Intelligent women like you have better lives here*, he wrote. *There is this school called MIT, the best science school on earth. You should try to get in at any cost.*

That didn't sound appealing to me. Restarting life in a foreign country at thirty? And what about Lanbo?

Really, it was quite funny when I thought about it: "go west" is a folk adage meaning "go to die," as Buddhists believe Paradise is in the west, which one can only reach in the afterlife. I placed the letter under my table lamp.

I was tired; I wanted to take a nap. Then I remembered tomorrow.

I had forgotten to tell Lanbo about my birthday. Men don't remember things like this. Maybe, just maybe, he would make an exception and spend this weekend with me?

I rolled off the bed and threw on a jacket. I ran out the door and down the stairs.

I hoped he was still in his office. At the public phone desk in a small retail store I dialed once, twice, and again. The cold metal dial was getting warm; still no one answered at the other end. The only sound was the stubborn long "du—, du—"…

I dragged my legs home. So he had left in the morning. He was already there by now, with his good-tempered wife and adorable young son. Tonight, he would attend to her lovingly.

My room was empty and cold. I couldn't bear it. I walked down to the street again, hoping to absorb some warmth from the bustle of the crowd.

Row upon row of retail clothing and merchandise stores were all piping music into the street to attract customers. The reform and the opening-up policy had made everyone thirsty for money. The entire city seemed devoted to private business now. I idled away my time here and there. Above a theater, a giant ad for the Russian movie *Moscow Doesn't Believe in Tears* bore down on me. Hanging on the sides of many store doors were opposing couplets written on scrolls of red paper, manufacturing a holiday atmosphere. It took me a few moments to remember this was September, 1987, and the 66th birthday of the Party was coming soon. What was there to celebrate?

At 2:30 pm I called again from another public phone. The familiar voice spoke after the first ring. For a moment all my misgivings gave way to joy.

"The mayor promised me an apartment," I said.

"Yeah, right," he said.

I paused. "Could you stay here tonight?" I asked softly. "Tomorrow is my birthday."

He was quiet.

"Please?"

"Sorry. No. Don't be too selfish. I try very hard to please both…Hello? Are you there?"

I was quiet.

"Hello?"

"Why not?"

"You know I'll be back Monday. All right?"

"How about Sunday night?" I backed up a step.

"Can't say. But don't feel bad. Actually, you can compute this for yourself

— I have been spending far more days with you than with her."

Slowly I put down the phone.

He wanted me to calculate the days? The store clerk stopped me as I was walking out. "Four *fen*!" she demanded. I dropped a handful of coins in her palm without counting.

So many people in the streets. From time to time a lone woman my age or slightly older — an *aged youth* — drifted toward me. More often I saw young couples with little boys. My gaze followed the boys long after they passed.

Counting who had gotten more days? I thought my reeducation had ended in the 70's. I thought love was so different from politics.

I wandered around until after seven. It was getting dark. By the time I got home, my parents were having supper. My younger sister was out with her boyfriend. My mother said they had waited for me for quite a while and she had kept my meal warm in the wok on the stove. "Come on quick, have supper with us," she called. My heart softened a bit. I said I had eaten, and walked into my bedroom without another look at them. I bolted the door from the inside and turned on my stereo: Shostakovich's *Seventh Symphony*, music both uplifting and heavyhearted, as if he had written it for me.

Next to the stereo, the neat pile of pages reminded me of the review meeting next week. Somehow, thinking of my model made me feel a bit reluctant to part from this world. But I quickly overcame this weakness.

The simplest way was to use the electrical outlet where my table lamp was plugged in, though I had to be very gentle — avoid making any noise that might frighten my parents. Even over the sound of my stereo, I could hear their small talk at the dining table.

I unplugged the lamp and measured my two little fingers against the holes in the outlet. Seemed the right size.

I stood and tried to think of anything I might need to take care of. Nothing came to mind. All right, I said to myself.

As my fingers touched the black plastic shell of the bell-shaped outlet, a thought floated into my mind. Since there was such an era as now, when stupid and pretentious women were the happiest, if only by chance, there should be another era in which a woman like me could have a good life. Yes, there would be such an era. There had to be one.

This thought delighted me so much that I withdrew my arms and grinned. Immediately I saw my slightly open mouth and happily curved facial lines in the mirror. My expression was inconsistent with the seriousness of whatever I was trying to do. As if I would be able to wait for that era to come! I closed my lips tight and knitted my eyebrows together, remembering Lanbo's comment that I looked prettiest when I wept or frowned. But I had no desire to weep right now. I was thinking only of how thrilling a motion it would be when my fingers, one from each hand, poked into the two black holes. In one move, just one move, the disordered electrons would form an orderly current between the positive and negative ends, with blue sparks starting from one finger, flowing through the heart, and closing the loop at the other finger. Then the oblivion of the west. The whole process probably would take less than a second, although I didn't know that for sure. Very simple, wasn't it? Just that simple like my first night with him, a moment I had regarded in the past as the most important, but hadn't it passed in a blink?

Right at this moment an uncontrollable desire throbbed from my lower body and surged up. My nakedness coincided with a man's so tightly there was no layer of air separating us. His powerful male end erected passionately in my unselfish and joyful containment — I wanted to go mad I wanted to cry I wanted to die. No moment ever provides higher satisfaction than this. The simplest, most primitive satisfaction. The man's face was an unknown one. But did that matter?

As I reached toward the outlet, my last worry was whether 220 volts were enough. In a clumsy move I knocked the unplugged lamp from the table and it clattered to the floor. My philosopher friend's letter was exposed where the lamp had been.

Go west.

Go West?

FEATHERS

On Wednesday, three uninvited messengers came.

That morning, ten-year-old Sail was bending her head low over the square dining table, concentrating on making a paper-cut of a scene from *The Red Detachment of Women*, the model ballet. A few weeks ago, Sail's big sister Jia, a Red Guard in the 3rd middle school, had brought home several paper-cut patterns, and the novel activity spread in the neighborhood like spring flu. With the same zeal they had collected Chairman Mao's photo buttons a year before, the kids now made, collected, and traded paper-cuts of everything: revolutionary heroes, flowers, animals, and landscapes. They showed off their collections to each other and competed. Regardless of their parents' political factions, the ones who collected the most patterns won the looks of admiration. Sail wanted to be the biggest collector of paper-cut art in the world.

Sail was home alone: Jia was in her school "doing revolution" and wouldn't be back until the weekend. Their little sister Windy had gone with Gaga, their grandmother, to the countryside, to hide from the armed fights between two factions of the Red Guards. Her father was at work — or more precisely, was under the scrutiny of the Revolutionary Rebellion Team. Her mother, a school principal with no functioning school to run, had gone to a grocery store before it opened, to ensure an up-front spot in the long line.

About eleven a neighbor peeked in the window. Sail glanced up and saw Uncle Luo, the head of the Revolutionary Rebellion Team. "Are you looking for my father?" she said. "He's not home yet." The man's eyes searched inside; he shook his head slightly and left without a word. There was something strange in his stern face.

About noon appeared three uninvited guests, all teenage girls of Jia's age. Sail recognized one who wore a Red Guard armband as Jia's close friend, nicknamed "Foreign Ginger" for her pale skin.

Sail jumped up, "Is my big sister coming home early?"

The three teenagers looked at each other, none eager to reply. Foreign Ginger said, "Where are your parents?"

"They're not home. I'm in charge," Sail said. "Does my big sister have a message for me then?"

Foreign Ginger said with great hesitation, "Your sister . . . she was wounded."

"How? How bad is it? Where is she now?"

"She is in the hospital. No, not too bad. We came to fetch your parents."

Sail exhaled in relief as her father walked through the door. All the girls fell silent again. "Sail, go to the dining hall and get lunch for our guests," her father said after greeting the teenagers.

Sail obediently put a pan and a couple of meal pails into a basket and walked out. The July sun was directly over her head, scorching and blinding. Nothing really bad could happen on such a bright day.

*

Sail's family lived on the bank of the Jialing River near to its confluence with the Yangtze, and downstream from the 3rd middle school in a northern suburb. The three daughters were baby-named Jia, Sail, and Windy, results of their mother's life-long romance with the river. When Mother gave birth to each, she looked out the hospital window, and used the first thing she saw for the baby's name. Jia was born in winter, and Mother saw nothing but the Jialing River itself. Sail was born in spring when boats crowded the water. Windy was the consequence of Mother's failed birth control. When baby Windy arrived in the world on a stormy summer day, Mother could hear nothing but the wind against the glass and see nothing but flying sand and rolling pebbles. The girls were 6 and 6 years apart in age, like the beginning of a neat number series. Between the oldest Jia and the youngest Windy, a recurrent cycle of 12 years of Earthly Branches was completed, so those two sisters shared the same animal symbol, Dragon, a respectful and worrisome Zodiac. Sail, on the other hand, was only an ordinary Monkey, with an ordinary face sandwiched between her two beautiful sisters. When she was little, Mother used to joke, Hey, was my Sail switched by the hospital?

Shortly after Jia's birth, Gaga arrived from the countryside to help take care of the baby. She adored the Little Jia so much that she stayed. How could she not? In her whole life she had given birth to thirteen children in a small village, and none, except Sail's mother, lived to see their first birthday. So Gaga began life a second time in the city, rearing one baby after another with great pleasure, while the babies' mother was constantly busy running a school district and working as principal.

Sail knew why Windy went with Gaga — because her little sister could not fall asleep without clutching at Gaga's flabby, empty bag breasts, Windy's security blanket. When Sail was little she too liked to sleep with Gaga; Gaga had this clean fragrant smell like no one else, because she used only the Chinese honey locust tree pods to wash clothes, as the concept of soap was too new for her to trust. But Sail did not know why Mother kept her in the city with bullets flying around day and night. She wondered, but she did not ask.

*

Fifteen minutes later Sail returned with steaming rice in the pan and a couple of dishes in each pail. She paused at the door: her father was crying, collapsed on Gaga's bamboo chaise. He never cried, not even when the Rebellion Team shamed him. He never sat on Gaga's chaise either.

Jia's friends were crying too. Sail quietly put down the lunch basket, took five bowls out of the cupboard, and spooned rice into each bowl. "Please have lunch," she said in a normal voice. No one answered.

She handed a bowl of rice and a pair of chopsticks to each visitor. To her father she gave his blue-white china bowl, slightly bigger than the others. He took it and placed it on the floor beside him without looking. Foreign Ginger had just popped a clump of rice into her mouth, but seeing Sail's father she put her bowl down beside the paper-cut of the woman soldier. The two other girls followed suit. The steam from the rice bowls wafted unattended; the girls avoided glancing at them.

Sail's father got up with effort and said to the girls, "If you don't want to eat, let's go to the school now."

"Am I going with you?" Sail said.

"No, you must wait for your mother. Tell her what happened and come with her."

With these words he took to his feet, and the three girls quietly followed him out. Sail watched them disappear through the door of the courtyard.

*

Alone, she waited for her mother; it was impossible to do her paper-cut now. Sail tried to eat a bit of rice, but could not swallow. She was not sure what had happened, and did not want it made clear. She went to the courtyard door and peered down the noisy road several times, but her mother was not among the crowds. She must have been in a long line waiting to be yelled at by the grocery store workers. These days a grocery store worker was like a queen.

Half an hour passed; Sail decided to go look for her mother. She wondered if she should lock her door with the "iron-general" lock. Didn't Gaga always lock the door when no one was left inside? She locked the door, put the key in her pants pocket, and went out to the street.

Two hours later Sail returned home exhausted, her shirt soaking in sweat and her wet hair stuck to her neck. She had gone to several stores and squeezed into every line to be cursed by frustrated grocery shoppers, but found no trace of her mother. At her door she gasped: the hasp and staple were pried out. Then she saw a grocery basket crushed on the ground, a few yellowed vegetable leaves littered around.

Aunt Tang, Uncle Luo's wife, approached, crossing the courtyard. "Your mama said, 'What a silly Sail, locking the door without leaving the key!'" Aunt Tang mimicked. "Then I told her, Jia is drowned, and she fell like this." Aunt Tang opened her arms to topple backward.

"You made that up!" Sail said.

"Yeee! Am I like one to make things up?" Aunt Tang raised her voice. But when she saw Sail's teeth bared like a cat, she stepped backward.

"The 3rd middle school called the office this morning! Your Uncle Luo answered the phone!" Aunt Tang said. Sail just stared at her. "Your mama's gone to your sister's school. Look at you. You better go wash your face."

Sail considered walking to Jia's school. She didn't have a penny, and she could not take the bus. But how many hours would it take to walk? Jia rarely took the bus when she came home on the weekend. She walked, to save money, and to learn from the Red Army's long march. "This is only a thousandth of the long march," Jia once said. Sail wished she had asked her big sister how many hours it took.

*

She lay on her bamboo mattress, closed her eyes, and tried to think. The mattress was cool at first, but soon became uncomfortably hot on every spot she rolled to. She did not like that gossipy neighbor. She did not like what she'd heard. Drowned and wounded were two different things. Or perhaps Jia fell into the river, and the river took her to some point downstream, near home, and good-hearted strangers rescued her. I should take a nap, she told herself, and let Big Sister wake me up when she returns home.

When she awoke, outside was dark and inside was quiet. She looked at the double horse-hoof alarm clock on the nightstand and saw it was five in the morning. She got up, thirsty and hungry. When she left her house she did not lock the door. It could no longer be locked. There were still stars in the sky, and an occasional small breeze, but the air was already working up toward another hot day. She walked to the Number 2 bus line, where she had seen Jia off four days before. A long line had already formed for the first bus, but the conductor selling tickets was half asleep. Sail waited until the bus was almost filled. She hid her small body between several impatient men and sneaked on without incident. The crowded bus took more than an hour to arrive at Sha'ping terminal.

Sail ran across the dusty suburban street to the gate of the 3rd middle school. Inside the gate she ran toward the larger-than-life statue of Chairman Mao. At the statue she turned right to the three-story classroom building. In the second floor's meeting room, she saw her parents sitting silently, surrounded by a crowd of teenage girls and boys. Mother's eyes were swollen like walnuts. When Sail appeared at the door, her parents stared like they didn't recognize her. There was no life in their faces. Sail looked around fiercely but did not see Jia anywhere.

"Where is my big sister?" she demanded.

Foreign Ginger emerged from the crowd, pulled her out to the hallway and whispered that Jia had already been buried the previous afternoon. The weather was too hot, she said.

"No—!" Sail screamed. "Where is she? I want to see her! I want to see her!"

Foreign Ginger started to weep. Sail charged into the meeting room again and shouted to Mother: "I want to see Big Sister! Take me to see her!"

Her father responded in a low roar: "Stop it! Your mother hasn't slept the whole night! Don't make her cry again!"

Then Sail heard Mother's trembling voice, "Sail, my child, your sister's coffin has been nailed. You can't see her any more."

"I am going to pry the coffin open!" Sail said. Mother choked with sobs, tears streaming down her cheeks like a broken chain of beads.

Foreign Ginger came up again and looked into Sail's eyes. "Little sister," she said earnestly, "Jia is a hero. She died for Chairman Mao."

Sail stared at her. So it was all right for Jia to die?

That day Foreign Ginger gave her Jia's diary. On the inside of the front cover was a hand-copied poem:

> "Life is precious
> Love is more so
> For my belief
> I let both go"

*

When Sail was little, four or five perhaps, Gaga used to tell her: Listen, *Cute*, if you dream of a dead person, if she asks you to go with her, don't. Sail would snuggle at Gaga's knees and ask, But, what if I like her?

Uh-uh, Gaga shook her furrowed cheeks, in the affectionate way she did. Not if you don't want to die, *Cute*.

Why don't I want to die, Gaga?

Your torso, hair and skin, are benefits from your father and mother. You die before they do, that is unfilial.

I'm filial to you, Gaga, Sail said eagerly.

Good girl. Gaga stroked Sail's hair, with her work-worn palm, callused like a lump of old ginger. Sail could hear the sizzle of the static on her hair.

But when Jia appeared in her dreams, no such question was ever posed. Jia kicked a shuttlecock made of rooster feathers, or jumped around a rubber rope while singing. It was Sail who ended up asking to go with her, wherever she was. Jia never answered; she just turned to mist, leaving Sail to wake to blankness.

*

Mother kept herself in bed most of the time. At her better moments she would sit up, empty-eyed, and repeatedly chatter: "I shouldn't have named her 'Jia' . . . then the Jialing River wouldn't have taken her back. . . ."

Or she would say with a blind smile: "What a strong child, like a calf..." as if Jia were still alive.

She kept all the windows in the house open, day and night. If Sail wanted to close them on a rainy day, Mother would scold, "Stop! How can your sister find a way to get back inside?"

Jia, in the meanwhile, found easy access to Sail's dreams.

No one told Sail how Jia died. From overheard words here and there, she pictured her sister swimming with Chairman Mao in the river, her shoulder-length black hair fading in and out of the brown waves.

*

A month after Jia's death, the Red Guard factions ceased fire. Gaga and Sail's little sister Windy returned home from the countryside. Mother managed to pull herself out of the river of grief she had sunk into, and took Sail to meet them at the port.

Gaga had brought with her big and small bags of red beans, green beans, broad beans, sweet potato chips, and sunflower seeds. Mother squeezed out a smile, said a few words of greeting, took the bigger bags, and handed a small one to Sail, then abruptly turned and walked ahead.

"What's your ma's hurry?" Gaga jolted along with her once-bound feet. Four-year-old Windy, cute as a doll with sun-reddened face, imitated Gaga like a parrot, "What's Mama's hurry?" and she sneaked a little hand into the bag of sweet potato chips. Gaga pulled her hand out and said, "Haven't you had enough? You little naughty! This is for your sisters." She turned to ask Sail, "Does your big sister come home this weekend?"

Sail pretended she didn't hear. She ran ahead and caught up with her mother and whispered. Mother said, "Whatever you do, don't tell Gaga. It'll kill her." Tears swelled up in her eyes.

"But…"

"Make up a story," Mother said. She sped up again and it was hard for Sail to keep the pace with her. The August sun was too bright, it hurt her eyes.

"What story, Mama?"

Mother stamped a foot. "Don't follow me so tight! Gaga'll suspect!"

Sail twisted her neck to see how far Gaga was behind; instead she was startled to meet the dark eyeballs of her baby sister. Windy stood right before her, sucking a thumb.

"I heard, I'm gonna tell," Windy babbled.

"Heard what? Tell what?"

"I heard, I heard!" Windy clapped hands and hopped around. "I tell Gaga, tell Big Sister!" Then she stood on toes and hissed, "But I won't if you give me a new flower dress."

Windy wanted a floral dress! As if this were a lollipop like other 4-year-olds wanted. Sail looked around a street full of pedestrians in gray, blue and military green, then glanced at her own patched, hand-me-down shirt. She was momentarily amused by Windy's request, a smile almost opened. Then she looked up and saw Mother's back hunched beneath many bags. Turning her head she saw 75-year-old Gaga behind them struggling to hurry with her inconvenient feet. Lowering her eyes she saw Windy's thumb in her mouth again, her mischievous eyes twinkling. What was Sail going to tell Gaga?

Many years later Sail realized that was the moment her childhood ended, in the hot and blood-stink summer of 1968. Her maturity began with a big lie, at the age of 10.

When they arrived at their courtyard door, a neighbor was already waiting. Aunt Tang greeted them eagerly by saying, "Gaga, I'm so sorry about Jia. . . ." And Sail interrupted, "You are sorry about my sister joining the army? Is this a reactionary view or what?" She steered Gaga toward home and Gaga sighed, "Even the neighbor knows I'll miss my Little Jia. You shouldn't be so rude to her good intention."

A flock of black crows landed on the roof. One made a raucous cry. "How inauspicious," Gaga said, "Someone dead nearby?" Sail shook her head like a rattle-drum. "No, no no no," she said.

That evening after Gaga went to bed early, tired after the long trip, Sail visited each and every family in the courtyard and told them the truth about her lie. Men shook their heads and opined various advice, while women wiped their moist eyes and promised to comply. But it was the children that worried Sail. She knew from now on she would have to keep an eye open even in sleep.

*

Before Gaga's return, Sail once eavesdropped on Mother sobbing out to a relative that, when she arrived at the school, Jia looked as if asleep, but as soon as Mother began calling her name, white foam seeped out of Jia's mouth. "She heard me, my poor daughter, she heard me. . . ." This seemed a sign to Sail that Jia did not really die; after all, Sail had never seen the body.

Sail began to look for Jia, on the streets, in stores, at mass meetings, as if fact and belief were unrelated notions. When she started middle school the next year, she spent months scrutinizing the faces of older girls in the noisy schoolyard. Only one made Sail pause: the girl's cheekbones were a bit prominent, like Jia's. She followed her everywhere: to her classroom, to the playground (where she jump-roped like Jia), to her bus station after school. The girl at first ignored Sail. Then one day she blocked Sail's way and exploded, "Do I have four arms or eight legs? Why do you always stare at me?"

Sail flinched and mumbled, "You look like my big sister." She showed her a photo, in which Jia wore a paramilitary uniform and held a book of Chairman Mao near her heart. The girl examined the photo and laughed, "You call that alike?" Then she looked at it again more closely and paused. "Hmm, she seems a bit like my cousin Xiaodi." They became friends after that. Her name was Yingbo, *reflection in the waves*.

Sail told Yingbo about her lie to Gaga that Jia had joined the army and was stationed in Xinjiang Province. Her new friend asked why Xinjiang. It's the farthest province from us, Sail told her, so Gaga can't find out. "That's weird," Yingbo said, "my cousin is also a soldier in Xinjiang." What she said did not surprise Sail. It actually gave her hope, in an inexplicable way.

*

One day in school Sail's class criticized the "Petofi Club," a counter-revolution movement in 1956 Hungary that almost overturned their Communist government and resulted in the Soviet Union's decisive intervention. The teacher seemed most angered that the counterrevolutionaries had fouled the name of the great 19th century Hungarian patriot poet, who had inspired many Communist heroes to give their lives to the revolutionary cause. He went on to recite a famous poem of Petofi's as an example:

"Life is precious
Love is more so
For our liberty
I let both go"

Sail now understood Jia had quoted Petofi in her diary, except one line didn't match. After class, she ran to find Yingbo and asked if she knew about the poem. "The teacher's version was right," Yingbo said positively. "Your sister just switched one line."

"But why?"

"Why? The Party already got us the liberty. It's politically incorrect to use that word now."

*

Every few weeks Sail wrote a letter in Jia's name and read it to Gaga. They sat down on the narrow sun porch of their apartment, Gaga lying on the weathered bamboo chaise, squinting in the spring, summer, or autumn sun. Windy stuck a bamboo-claw into Gaga's collar and scratched her back, and Gaga sighed with joy, "What a luxury, what a luxury." Then she fell into an attentive quietness as Sail cut open the glued envelope. Illiterate Gaga had great respect for the written word. She nodded every so often to what Sail was reading, and each nod gave Sail warm encouragement, while Windy ran around Gaga's chaise and Sail's wooden stool. It was almost a perfect, happy scene, except Mother neither read nor listened to the letters Sail wrote. As for Sail herself, at times she believed the letters were real. More real than Jia's death.

Sometimes Gaga asked questions such as Xinjiang Province's weather and customs, whether Jia was kept warm and well fed, or whether there were battles along the borders between China and the Soviet Union. But the letters never reported anything bad.

Everything went well for two years; by then the letters began to "arrive" more sparsely, but unsuspicious Gaga only sighed occasionally, "When the bird's wings grow hard, she's no longer attached to the roost." Then, one day after Gaga chatted with a neighbor, she said to Mother, "Old Wang's boy came home for vacation. Isn't it a time for Jia's visit too?" Mother hurried to do things and left the question unanswered, only throwing Sail a glance.

*

Sail had never prepared for such a question. She drilled her brain so hard that she got a headache, still she couldn't come up with an answer. She wished Jia were there to supply her with a brilliant idea, as she often had before. For days Sail wore a sulking face in school and at home, until Yingbo asked what was wrong. Sail told her friend the quandary. Yingbo said, "How hard could that be? Let my cousin come disguised as your sister!" It turned out that Yingbo's cousin, Xiaodi, *morning flute*, was due for a visit home soon. Sail thought about Gaga's aging eyes, how recently she had asked Sail to thread the needle every time before mending clothes. Yingbo's idea might work. The only thing Sail worried was whether Xiaodi would go along.

*

Xiaodi showed up several weeks later. The day before, when Gaga heard Jia was coming home, she made fermented glutinous rice, her specialty and Jia's favorite. She steamed a pot of sweet rice, and fanned the rice with a round cattail leaf non-stop. After it was cooled, she thumbed a hole in the middle and put in a granule of yeast made in her hometown. Then she covered the pot, wrapped it in a thick quilt, and placed it in a closet. Windy followed her every single step. "At this time tomorrow it will be ready," Gaga said, "but we have to boil it before eating." Windy smacked her lips.

The next morning, when Gaga opened the pot, a sweet wine fragrance filled the room, but her smile faded in an instant: a third of the raw fermented glutinous rice was gone. Sail and Gaga found 7-year-old Windy drunk in her bed, unconscious. "What's to be done?" Sail cried out. Gaga shook Windy's limp body, "Wake up, my little ancestor, wake up." Sail knew Gaga was as scared as she was then — Gaga only called a child *ancestor* in anxiety. The next moment, Windy opened eyes and sat up and pointed to the door: "A woman soldier!"

Xiaodi walked in then. For a moment Sail thought she saw her big sister, the soldier she imagined when composing Jia's letters. Xiaodi's back was so straight, like a steel beam. Short hair tossed neatly into the green cap with a bright red star insignia, she walked in big strides. Windy jumped off her bed and shouted: "Woman soldier! Woman soldier!"

Gaga's eyes squinted at the sudden sunrays pouring in from the open door: "Is that my Little Jia? Is that my Little Jia?"

"But she's not my big sister," Windy shouted into Gaga's ear.

Sail froze. She just realized her mistake: she had not thought Windy would remember their big sister.

Xiaodi scooped at Windy. She smoothed Windy's silky black hair and said, "Hello, little Windy."

"How do you know my name?" Windy said.

Xiaodi smiled. "Isn't this how your big sister calls you? I'm her friend," she said. Oddly, her smile looked sad. Was this because of Jia? Sail wondered.

Gaga cupped Xiaodi's hand and said, "You are Little Jia's friend?"

"Yes," Xiaodi said. "How are you, Grandmother? Jia asked me to see you for her."

"Why doesn't she come home?"

"She's too busy, Grandmother," Xiaodi said. "She's been promoted and has big responsibilities."

"My Little Jia is a commander now?" Gaga sobbed.

"Yes, Grandmother, she is an excellent commander."

"Sit down, sit down, girl, tell me more about my Little Jia."

They sat, like grandmother and granddaughter, and chatted about Xinjiang and army life. Sail served boiled rice wine and fried sunflower seeds, while Windy offered Xiaodi her only candy. At one point Gaga told Xiaodi what nice letters Jia always wrote home and Sail saw Xiaodi's eyebrow leap. Gaga had kept the most recent letters under her pillow; now she asked Sail to show them to Xiaodi.

When Xiaodi was leaving, the sun was almost set. Sail walked her outside of the courtyard door and thanked her. Windy followed them like a tail.

"You could be a good writer," Xiaodi said to Sail.

"Who wants to be a writer?" Sail said. Writers were the lowest social class then — the "stinky ninth."

Xiaodi looked at her, and again Sail saw dejection in her pretty eyes, inconsistent with her soldierly bearing. Sail was no longer sure where this sadness had come from.

"*I* am a writer," Xiaodi said matter-of-factly. Sail was surprised — she didn't know the army had writers. Xiaodi turned, her soldier's big strokes creating a flutter. Quickly she was disappearing from Sail's sight. "Big Sister!" Sail called out.

Xiaodi's steps halted. Sail ran to her; Windy chased Sail. "Are you coming back?" Sail asked, eyes foggy.

Xiaodi said sternly, "Your sister wanted you to be a soldier too, didn't she?" She was quoting from a letter by Jia — Sail. "A soldier sheds blood but not tears," she added.

Sail rubbed eyes with the back of her hand. "I never cry," she said angrily.

Xiaodi's voice softened. "I know. You are a brave girl. I'm not your sister. You know that, don't you?"

Sail had to ask one more question that had been in her mind for quite awhile, and she did not know whom else to ask. "Is my sister a hero?"

Xiaodi hesitated, then said, "There are things beyond heroism. You'll understand when you grow up."

Windy galloped between them, like an alerted little dog, neck steered in one direction and then another, sniffing at the bigger girls. Sail grabbed her baby sister's chubby hand and said, "Let's go home." But Windy stood stubbornly, her black eyes fixed on Xiaodi's face.

Xiaodi said softly, "Little Windy, see you again, okay?" Sail took Windy to go home, her little sister looking back at Xiaodi.

Back at home, Sail heard Windy asking Gaga, "Why didn't my real big sister come home?" The question was like a hand gripping Sail's heart. She held her breath until Gaga said, "*Cute*, your big sister will be home someday."

Gaga always called her grandchildren *Cute*, beginning with Jia.

*

But the danger of exposure always hovered nearby. Rat, Uncle Luo's son, a year older than Windy, had a crush on the little girl. One day the two kids had a fight over a fledgling fallen off the roof. Windy saw the hopping bird first but Rat captured it. Windy said it was her bird and Rat said it was his. A moment later Windy came home all teary, telling Sail, "Rat said my big sister is a swollen log in the river!" Sail covered her little sister's mouth and looked around, relieved to see Gaga wasn't inside. She offered Windy to play with her paper-cuts, and Windy refused; she offered to tell Windy a story, and Windy refused. Sail wished she could give her sister a toy or candy, but there was neither in the house. Nor in the stores. Windy kept crying and Sail could not afford to let Gaga hear Windy repeat Rat's words.

She thought of a trick Jia had once told her: if you stretch out your arm, with rice in your open palm, and shut your eyes tight, sparrows will come to peck at the rice in your hand. Then if you close your fingers quick, you'll catch a bird. Sail had never tried this trick herself. She shushed Windy, went out to the courtyard, and opened both arms to stand like a scarecrow. Sure enough, soon a couple of sparrows came down from the roof and hovered around the rice in her open hands.

"Why are your eyes closed, sister?" Windy asked.

Sail opened her eyes to signal Windy to be quiet, and right at the moment a smart sparrow pecked a grain of rice from her hand and flapped away. Windy laughed and shouted, "Again, birdie, again!" Rat ran out of his door and watched, his little sparrow connected to his thumb by a thread. He offered to let Windy play with the sparrow, and Windy flopped to him and forgot about Sail. Sail thought of Rat's words, the swollen log in the river — was that what kids say about her big sister? Her heart ached and ached, an unlikely pain in such a young chest.

*

An inconceivable thing occurred the next day. Early in the morning, the whole courtyard was awakened by loud twitters. The power line above Rat's window was covered with a dense mass of sparrows, screaming at the top of their lungs. The fledgling's tender chirp echoed from inside Rat's house, one sound following another. Neighbors stood watching and commenting in amusement, and excited children threw pebbles at the birds. The sparrows dispersed, gathered, dispersed again, and gathered again. Each time fewer returned, and the human onlookers gradually dissipated. By the end of the day, only two sparrows remained, and they could not stop crying.

"Poor papa-mama. Poor baby," Gaga sighed.

Sail went to Rat. "They are the parents," she said to the boy, "why don't you give the baby bird back to them?"

"It's mine!" Rat said.

Aunt Tang, Rat's mother, made a tongue click. "Yeee," she said, "who are you to scold my boy? Can't you see he has nothing to play with at all? Are you as cold-hearted as your capitalist father, asking my son to give up his only toy?"

Across the courtyard, Sail's mother called sternly, "Sail! Back home right this instant!"

*

The parent sparrows stayed on the power line one day after another. They kept crying, though their voices got smaller and smaller. Windy went to Rat's house every day to check on and feed rice to the fledgling. Sail spent a good part of each day staring at the two crying sparrows. At last, one morning, they did not come back. Sail ran to Rat and asked to see the bird, but Rat refused.

She knew the fledgling was dead then. She ran to the courtyard's garbage pit and found a pinch of sparrow feathers wrapped in a newspaper. Just feathers. She took the feathers home. She folded up a little box with white paper, and put the feathers in the box. She cut a strip of cardboard and wrote on it

鸟之基

— *monument of bird*. She found a palm size spot of open soil in a corner of the courtyard and buried the box. After setting up the paper monument, she stood pondering how to explain everything to Windy. It would be another difficult moment. Yet she knew now it would come and pass like any point in time, regardless of her own turmoil, so she might as well treat it as fictional. #

MEN DON'T APOLOGIZE

1.

Each time a prospective suitor swerved away from Ou Hong, her father couldn't help but remind her to warm the hues of her face a little. He would clumsily jest, "Have they borrowed your rice and repaid with chaff?" And he always got the rebuttal, "Where do you think I got my hues from?" Those words choked off the even-tempered old man, once an eloquent teacher of Marxist-Leninist doctrine. He would quietly lament the metamorphosis of his sweet little girl, while she did what she pleased.

Ou Hong's mother had died shortly after the end of the Cultural Revolution. As if she could not manage the tremendous relief of waking up from a decade-long nightmare, her nerves just snapped like a string drawn too taut. Ou Hong was a freshman then, and her mother's last words were like a prophecy, that she, Ou Hong, would find a suitor among neighborhood boys, someone she was familiar with from childhood. The unsaid words: someone who wouldn't mind her aloofness and chronic sarcasm.

No one knew if the mother had a particular boy in mind, and Ou Hong took the prophecy as no more than a loving mother's kind wish. Four years passed and when graduation time came, Ou Hong was the only girl in her Mechanical Engineering class who had not been paired. On a campus of mostly male students she dated few, and never for very long. She departed university with the crown of "cold-eyed princess."

Then, in the spring, on her first day of work at the Bus Factory, she ran into a neighbor from childhood, to whom she hadn't uttered a word for 16 years, though she had seen him on TV and around home sometimes.

She was passing workers crowded around two TV cameramen inside the factory's gate, when a strangely familiar voice glued her feet to the ground. It came from a young man wearing a gray-striped western suit, freely and elegantly unbuttoned. His thin lips moved swiftly over a microphone while the overflowing light from his enthusiastic eyes swept through the audience. The mannerisms were his trademark as the host of the popular TV program, *Focal Interview*. He cast a look on Ou Hong before she could lurch away.

"Hey, look who's here." He turned off the microphone and said, "mountains don't circle but waters do." His long, girlish eyelashes flapped, as he contemplated the white dress-shirt tucked into her red jeans.

"What a white swan," he eulogized.

"Was I an ugly duckling before?" Ou Hong said. Immediately she bit her lip.

"No, no, I was," he said, in the charming self-deprecating tone that had made him adorable to his massive female audience. His voice and smile tore open every little detail of that autumn day in her childhood. She could hear — with a sharp clarity — her own flustered and exasperated voice shrieking, "One day! One day . . ." and see him bouncing backward, turning with a sinister smile, then disappearing around a corner of the wall.

What had she tried to say that day? As they stood face to face once again, 16 years condensed into 16 seconds. She felt on the verge of recovering those words, before they slipped away like water — shapeless, with nothing to grip. *One day* what? All these years of time were like beach sand, layer over layer, with unspoken words buried beneath, till unearthing became hopeless, yet she could not give up digging.

His lilting voice encroached, "What are you doing here anyway, white swan?"

She strutted away without another word. Her heart churned with anger as she sped to the Administration Building. Didn't he remember anything? How could he speak to her with such a casual intimacy?

2.

Chen Yiping was the neighbor boy's name, and the Political Institute was their neighborhood. The last time she spoke to him was 1966. He was 10. She was 8, until then a spoiled little princess pampered by her father's colleagues and students.

The Political Institute's function was to educate the Nationalist army's ex-generals, who surrendered, or fled unsuccessfully, when the victory of the Chinese Communists became inevitable in 1949. Ou Hong's father was the president of the Institute. He wore a four-pocket navy cadre uniform and lectured on revolutionary theory in a dignified manner, and those ex-generals were knocked out with admiration. His ability and excellent work even received recognition from Chairman Mao himself; the Great Leader received him in the People's Hall in Beijing and shook hands with him, a rare honor.

The Institute, located on the south side of the city, was housed in what was once the American Embassy, taken over by the new government after the American imperialists "ran away with their tails between their legs," as the popular song "Socialism Is Good" goes. In the garden-like Institute, Ou Hong's family had the entire second floor of a beautiful Western-style, two-story beige house, while two families of her father's subordinates shared the downstairs, one of these the Chen family.

That day in early fall of 1966 was an ordinary day; the sky was blue, the clouds were white, and the bird songs were jubilant. Ou Hong returned home from her elementary school uncertain whether she should be happy or upset about the classes stopping. Yiping slid down from a mulberry tree right in front of her, his lips purpled by the ripe berries.

"Brother," she said, "you scared me!" Girls and boys didn't talk at school, but in one's own yard the rules were relaxed.

"Who's your brother!" The boy hooted, surprising her in a big way.

Yiping was nicknamed by his schoolmates as a "sissy" and had never raised his voice at her or anyone before.

"Did you eat the wrong medicine this morning?" she teased.

"Your Pa ate the wrong medicine." The boy backed up a step and announced, "*The revolutionary situation is grand, and is getting better and better*. Your Pa is a loser, my Pa is in power now!"

"What do you mean?" Ou Hong said.

Yiping backed another step and ran away.

Puzzled, she walked to her father's office building. Long and dense green vines of ivy coated the walls; in front was a goldfish pond with stone rails. Pink lotus flowers bloomed graciously in the pond. She dallied at her favorite mossy-rimmed pond from which a dragonhead spurted water, but a surge of collective shouting from inside the building washed over her like a wave. Scampering through the front gate, she climbed up the rosewood stairs to the third floor, where the President's Office was located. She stood stunned at the wide open door: the usually neat and roomy office was a total mess, white papers with black and red print scattered everywhere. Her father was nowhere to be seen.

Another sharp wave of shouts erupted from the first floor. Ou Hong ran downstairs. Standing behind rows upon rows of sitting people, she saw her father on his knees in the center of the stage, the same stage where he would give long speeches and receive loud applause from the same crowd he faced now. Uncle Chen, her father's amiable subordinate, the kind neighbor of her family, the caring father of her playmate Yiping, pressed her father's head down till it almost touched the floor, his other hand holding a tall, pointy dunce cap made of cardboard. On the paper cap's surface was a column of hand-written, black ink characters, each bigger than the one above: *Capitalist Roader Ou.*

"Put the cap on your head!" Uncle Chen ordered. Kneeling prone, her father raised unsteady hands over his head and put on the dunce cap.

"Tell us you are a capitalist roader!"

"I am a capitalist roader," the small voice did not sound like her father's at all.

"Louder!"

"I am a capitalist roader!"

"You are a monster and demon!"

"I am a monster and demon. . . ."

As the revolutionary masses burst into loud bellowing "Bombard capitalist roaders!" and "Burn the monsters and demons!" Ou Hong sprinted through the meeting hall's passageway, blasting up to the stage, swirling white papers around her. Bending over, she butted her head into Uncle Chen's unsuspecting stomach, staggering the big man. Her shriek echoed in the meeting hall, "I won't let you bully my Papa!"

Uncle Chen caught his balance: "Little Hong, children are not allowed here. Revolution is a grownup matter."

She kicked him in the shins and screamed, "*You* are a monster and demon! My Papa is a good man!"

At that moment her father twisted his head toward her, struggling to look up from the floor with bloodshot eyes. "Get out, go home!" His husky voice was muffled, with nothing remaining of his usual dignified bearing. When she did not obey, Uncle Chen nodded to a thick-waisted woman who came up and pulled her out of the meeting hall, as Ou Hong kicked and cursed with the few dirty words she knew.

Once out the door, the woman whispered, "Go home; you'll only make things worse for your father." Her voice was surprisingly concerned, which was what made Ou Hong obey.

The upset girl ran into Yiping again. The boy kept a few feet from her and said:

"Yay, what did I say?"

"You are wrong! Your father is wrong! My Papa is not a capitalist roader!"

"He is too!" the boy clapped his hands and sang:

"Your Pa is a loser,
My Pa is a winner!"

As he sang, he jumped up and down on a pile of coal against his kitchen wall. Ou Hong said hurriedly, "Listen to me, Yiping, one day you—" Before her next word was out, *pa*! a charcoal briquette hit her forehead. The briquette shattered into thousands of particles, blacking her cheeks and blinding her eyes.

Compared to the episodes that followed later, the pain caused by the charcoal was really nothing. However, this was her first experience with humiliation, and the anguish, confusion and frustration had hit enormously. She kept rubbing her eyes, wanting to speak, as if completing the interrupted sentence was the most important thing at that moment, as if it was a lifebuoy for her sunken body, "One day, one day—" Her words broke to sobbing, as Yiping ran away in victory.

Her father returned home that evening, weary and exhausted but in one piece, with no apparent physical wounds. His spirit had yet to be broken completely. That happened days later, in a house raid conducted by outside Red Guards who seized everything he treasured. Compared to those middle school teenagers, Uncle Chen and his people were rather merciful. The following week, the news came from Ou Hong's elementary school, that her principal had been beaten to death by Red Guards from a nearby middle school. Not until years later, when she was older, did she realize how lucky her father had been during the cruelest initial months of the Cultural Revolution. Even when she was mature enough to admit that her father's actions were no more than strategic self-protection, perhaps mixed with confusion, and the traditional virtue of "enduring humiliation in order to discharge important duties," she could never bear to look back at that day, or look straight into her father's eyes.

Following her father's disgrace, she became a "fallen phoenix less than a chicken," being constantly bullied by the neighborhood boys. The boys also smashed the artful stone dragonhead adorning the pond, and killed all the goldfish. As she grew up, her memory of almost all of that would fade; what never went away was the picture of her father on his knees, placing the dunce cap on to his own head with unsteady hands. It was an impossible scene — worse because at that young age she could not understand what was being crushed in her image of man. It was not because of what they did to him, nor what they did to her; it was he, her father, what *he did* that day. How could a revolutionary hero, who had never yielded to the enemy's torture and death threats, become such a pitiful man when facing his own comrades and those he had liberated? The answer was beyond her. Each time the denunciation scene resurfaced, she would shudder, and shake her head rapidly to get rid of the terrible image. She never talked about this to anyone, her parents or friends. She just let the anguish mold her insides — and the hues on her face — over time.

She never again spoke to Uncle Chen, who for a while became the number one leader of the Revolutionary Rebellion in the Political Institute. Not even after she learned that he was the one who warned her father about the Red Guards' house raid, not even a decade later when both men returned to their original posts — her father again the president of the Institute and Uncle Chen his subordinate. She did not speak to Yiping either; not when they went to the same middle school, not after she went to university and he became the city's most popular TV program host and a rising star.

3.

In the north of the city, at the Bus Factory built of gray concrete and devoid of anything green, Ou Hong's arrival puzzled many. What was a university graduate doing here? No man (not to mention a woman) with a university degree had worked at the factory in its 30 years of history. Even the Chief Engineer and the Director of the Technical Division only had a secondary specialty school diploma.

Now Ou Hong understood why the Political Advisor in her university had smiled at her handsomely. She must have helped his mission involuntarily and enormously. This January, her campus had once again been filled with the same red slogans, *Go to the Most Needy Place of Our Motherland!* As if it were still the 50s or 60s, and they, the post-Cultural Revolution students, were still taken in by those big words and wouldn't beat out each other's brains to compete for the best jobs. The same tradition from before the Ten Disastrous Years (as the Cultural Revolution was called now) continued: everyone was required to fill the Graduation Assignment Volunteer Form, and was allowed three choices. Ou Hong didn't actually care where she went, but she thought a little of her father's frost-like hoary temples, and a rare moment of softness came over her. She knew her father would like her to stay in the city, although she hadn't asked — didn't want to ask — for his advice. She scanned the list of local jobs, and the Bus Factory caught her eye. The factory name revived a latent memory, and she felt a sudden urgency to complete a personal mission: she must find Master Liu, a man from her past. She made the Bus Factory her first option, and got the assignment nobody else wanted.

She chose to start her three-month probation in the Chassis Shop because the foreman's surname was Liu.

Liu Huagu was a typical southern man in his late 20s, of average height, with a swarthy complexion, a wide forehead, and delicate cheekbones. If there was any deficiency in his mien, it was that he looked at everybody out of the corner of his eye, making you feel denigrated.

When Ou Hong arrived, Liu Huagu was lighting a cigar on the blinding white flame of a welding torch held in the hand of his apprentice, "Mynah." Liu Huagu's bony hand flicked like a snake's forked tongue. Before Ou Hong realized what he had been doing, the cigar, flashing tiny red sparks, was already hanging between his teeth. Behind him, on the workshop's wide wall, a large sign bore down on them, "Smoking Prohibited."

"How hot is the flame of the welding torch?" she asked nonchalantly.

"Hmm?" The cigar fuzzed Liu Huagu's tongue. "Over 3000° C," he answered, somewhat taken aback, and then said, " 'Ou' is an unusual surname."

"Certainly not as common as Liu." Her gaze dwelled on his face for a second too long — it bore no resemblance to the other Master Liu. She weighed the bluntness of her next question, but asked anyway.

"Master Liu—" she felt a bit strange to call such a young man *master* — "does your father work here too? Was he once a member of the Workers Propaganda Team?"

Liu Huagu leered at her. "What, checking my eight generations?"

"Never mind then," she said.

The foreman turned to his apprentice. "Mynah, what work do we have for Miss University?"

"Master, are you kidding? In this shop even the rats are all male!" The young man at his side fleered, lifting up a 12-pound hammer and pounding at random on an open chassis with a loud *Bang*.

Liu Huagu flung open his hands at Ou Hong, "Help yourself. See what you can do."

Amidst the loud din of metal colliding, she walked in circles around the half-assembled chassis, trying to figure out her position. All the while she felt Mynah's eyes following her. At one point she stopped to survey an old worker's face, then shook her head and continued circling. In the third circle she heard Mynah say, "His mother's! Aren't men and women equal? Can I take a break too, Master?"

"Nobody'll think you're a mute if you shut up," Liu Huagu said.

Ou Hong sauntered over to Mynah, who was shooting a rocker arm with the blaze of his welding torch, and asked:

"How often do our buses have accidents?"

"Huh?" *Bang!* Mynah hammered the heated rocker arm. "How inauspicious!"

"How long have you been doing this?"

"Doing *what?*" Mynah did not stop hammering.

"Do you know that the rocker arm is made of chilled steel?"

"Em?"

"Never mind," Ou Hong said, and resumed her circling. But Mynah wasn't exactly dumb. He yelled at her back: "You have a problem with my way, Miss University? Tell you what, my master taught me this, and my master's master taught him this. Know who my master's master is? It's Manager Gao!"

"Whatever," Ou Hong said.

The next morning Ou Hong did not report to the Chassis Shop. She wandered through the adjoining Bus Body Shop and the Trial Model Shop, then to the Supply and Marketing Division, and the Personnel Division, everywhere checking on faces. No one knew what she was doing; the entire factory did not seem to know how to handle this newcomer. There were speculations: some workers whispered she might be appointed as an inspector.

At one time, in the Bus Body Shop, after Ou Hong checked an old man's face and the man ignored her, she stooped next to him, while he squatted on a large iron sheet and skillfully hammered it. For quite a while, she watched with amusement the iron sheet bouncing rhythmically under his nimble hammer, the cambered surface of a bus front unfolding. Finally she said, "So our bus is hand-made."

"Is there another way?" The old worker replied, not lifting his eyes.

The factory had a small number of women employees, who held jobs such as clerks, nurses, and typists. It was those women who started to stir the waiting air. Gossip began to circle around. Ou Hong's unwrinkled white shirt, contrasting with her scarlet red jeans, was a loud violation of the factory's all-blue "labor protection uniform" dress code, which did not help. Nor did her slender waist and long legs.

Liu Huagu overheard a conversation between two typists in the administration office.

"The foxy girl is after a boyfriend," one woman whispered.

"A worker? Why would she want one?"

"Maybe she had bad grades in college."

"Better watch your man closely."

Liu Huagu went to find the wandering girl and brought her back to the Chassis Shop.

"Don't cause me to lose face," he warned her.

"*Your* face?"

"Do whatever you want after you finish here. Right now I'm your master."

He took her to his small make-shift room, a cubbyhole with shelves for walls and a cloth door, threw her a set of blue coveralls, and said, "Make yourself look like a proper worker!" Despite his leering eye, his tone was that of a concerned elder brother: This hit her soft spot and she obeyed. After she came out, she went to find a lightweight hammer, and started to work with the men.

It did not take long for her to notice Liu Huagu's unexpected personal charm and power over the other workers, especially his apprentices. Even the glib-tongued Mynah was always ready to take his orders. Somehow he had bought them over, she figured. She noticed that every day, at exactly 12 o'clock, Liu Huagu told Mynah to stop work and go for lunch. By the time Ou Hong and other workers arrived to long lines in the dining hall, Mynah had already wolfed down half of the rice in his white-tin meal box.

Several weeks passed and Ou Hong hadn't being able to find any information about the Master Liu she was looking for. It made it that much more difficult that she didn't know his given name. During the two years when she saw him every weekday, she'd never thought to ask. How could she know? She was only a middle school student then and had always called him Master Liu.

The chassis assembly work was tedious, and she quickly became bored with it. Looking around, she couldn't figure out why the workers were so content. The tool they liked the most was the 12-pound hammer. Here didn't fit, *Bang*! There didn't fit, *Bang*! No machines other than the overhead crane. If several *Bang*s still didn't work, they turned on a welding torch and heated the particular parts to red, softening the stubborn and unruly steel, and then hammered again. No one was concerned that the high temperature might weaken those parts made of chilled steel and cause them to fracture later. Still, you had to admire the fact that all the buses in the city and its surrounding counties — a population of over 10 million — came from their bare hands.

What was an engineer needed for in such a backward place? Soon Ou Hong started to scheme about changing her job. Although she knew that switching jobs was harder than landing on the moon, she had one dim hope: several of her schoolmates hating their job assignments had been talking about running a private placement center, the first in the city. They were trying to make it a legal activity. If that didn't work out, the last resort would be her father, though she hated to ask for his help. He had connections everywhere.

Then a series of episodes stalled her plans.

4.

Mynah the glib-tongue turned out to be very easy to please. Almost as soon as the oversized blue-canvas labor-uniform covered Ou Hong's graceful curves and made her look the same as everyone else, he started to offer her a helping hand. When he saw it didn't take her too long to manage the 12-pound hammer (though she refused to have anything to do with the welding torch), Mynah cursed fewer "his mother's" in her presence.

Ou Hong's coldness toward the popular TV guy further pleased him, as if that handed him an advantage.

Yiping came to the Bus Factory a few more times, alone and without the camera, looking for Ou Hong. Each time Mynah spotted him, he ran back and told Ou Hong, who immediately hid in Liu Huagu's cubbyhole.

Yiping always looked in the Administration Building first, certain that he was in the right place each time. He shook hands with Manager Gao who asked for more TV promotion of the Bus Factory; he waved to his female fans, who pressed their faces flat on the window and stared at him, with no less enthusiasm than the first time. Yiping, of course, did not find Ou Hong there. When he eventually came to the Chassis Shop, Ou Hong slid to the adjoining Bus Body Shop. By the time he traced her to the Bus Body Shop, she had gone to the Public Health Office. The hide-and-seek went on for almost an hour, until Yiping ran short of patience. The last time, he left a note written with calligraphy like dragons flying and phoenixes dancing, taped on the Chassis Shop's gate. It read, "White swan, don't hide from love!" When Mynah asked Ou Hong what to do with it, she tore it off, crumpled it and dropped it on the floor. As this made her the center of the factory's gossip again, the workers in the Chassis Shop became increasingly protective of her, not much different from a family of brothers taking care of their baby sister. Even Liu Huagu didn't leer at her anymore.

One Friday, Mynah asked her a bit cryptically if she wanted to go with them on a road test Sunday.

"On a weekend?" Ou Hong wondered if this was another trick they played to make overtime bonuses.

"Well, not exactly work."

He told her, with some hemming and hawing, they were going to a far suburb for a spring outing ("To step on the greens," he said) in the name of a road test. Not exactly a cheat, he quoted his master's words, because they worked six days a week and had no vacations.

When Ou Hong showed up on Sunday morning, Liu Huagu appeared surprised. He goggled at each worker, and no one said a word. In the end he involuntarily waved her on to the newly finished bus.

That day turned out to be a treat. Away from the heavily polluted city, they drove and stopped, entertaining themselves with the ravishing spring landscapes. Then they had a picnic in a farming village, where fragrant gardenia bloomed profusely. The villagers gladly slaughtered a pig for their lunch and sold them live chickens and fresh farm goods. The rustic meal made everyone dispense with formalities, and they derided and taunted, and laughed up a storm. For the first time in a long while, Ou Hong loosened up completely, and let herself enjoy such a rare moment, as jovial as animals at large in nature, with no need to consider her choice of words or manner. Perhaps because of the fresh air and food (or because Mynah and the other workers kept putting food in her bowl), she also ate a lot more than usual. By the time they started home, everyone was stuffed, and their shoulders and arms were fully loaded with fresh vegetables, live chickens and eggs, even sweet-rice cakes.

Spring evenings come early, and it was soon dusk. The inspector driving the bus grew a bit impatient, and he shifted into fourth gear. At one point Liu Huagu, who sat right behind the driver, cringed as he listened to the chassis, but everything sounded normal. The bus slowed down making a hard right turn. Following an aberrant swerve, the bus suddenly bounced, and everyone's butt sprang from their seats. Backpacks and baskets slid to one side, hitting whatever was in their way. The bagged chickens cackled all at once, and someone cried, "Oh my eggs!" Between the noises, the front wheels of the bus rubbed the road to an ear-stabbing squeal as the driver trampled the brake all the way to the floor. The front of the bus disobediently threw itself to the left side of the road, smacking the rocky cliff, and then sank into a ditch.

Ou Hong had been sitting by a window, and her forehead bumped against the glass. For a few seconds she felt disoriented. She touched her forehead and was relieved to find just a little round lump.

Liu Huagu managed to push open the middle passenger door on the right side of the bus, and directed everyone to get off. Fortunately, no one was seriously hurt. They split up into groups and searched up and down the road but found no villages or shops nearby, and lost all hope of finding a telephone. They gathered around Liu Huagu, who told them to hitchhike back to town, and send a tow truck the next morning. He himself would stay and guard the bus overnight.

This gave rise to a flurry of discussion and disagreement, and all wanted to stay with him.

"Think about it, brothers," Liu Huagu said, "you want the management to see our mess?" He pointed to the ditched bus where chicken cackles continued sporadically. "Just take your groceries home and enjoy before they cause any trouble for me."

"I am staying with you no matter what, Master." Mynah said with a smile.

Liu Huagu frowned. Before he opened his lips Mynah raised his shoulder bag, "Don't worry, Master, I'm all prepared."

Ou Hong hadn't said a word; she kept glancing under the bus. Now that Mynah had gotten his way she stopped hesitating. She asked, "Anyone got a flashlight?"

No one did.

"Don't worry," a worker said, "there's the moonlight."

Liu Huagu leered at her as to say, "Who could have prepared everything for you, Miss University?"

"I must stay too," Ou Hong said, "I have a theory and I need to check the chassis the first thing in the morning, before the tow truck arrives."

The workers looked at each other, not knowing how to react.

Mynah smiled resplendently at Ou Hong, who was in her white shirt and red jeans again today, and said, "Not afraid of a tiger eating you?"

"Would you let that happen?" she said to Mynah, eyeing Liu Huagu.

To her surprise, Liu Huagu did not insist on her leaving with the others.

After seeing off their co-workers, the three climbed up on a small hill above the bus. Liu Huagu went into the woods, returned with an armful of withered tree branches and set a campfire. ("Ahh," Ou Hong said, "You *are* a handy man." "My master was an 'insert' in the countryside for eight years," Mynah said.) Ou Hong watched the branches pitter-pattered in red yellow flames. The two men smoked. In this wild place with no village ahead and no tavern behind, the spring night was incredibly quiet. Once in a while a truck passed by, its headlight sweeping over the ditched bus, and the sight seemed to slow the truck, but not enough to make it stop. The night wind brought a chill, and they crowded closer to the fire and to each other.

"Miss University," Mynah broke the silence, "why don't you tell us a story? You must've read lots of books."

Ou Hong searched through her memory for interesting books involving workers, but found few. "I once read an American novel called *Wheels*," she said after a hesitation.

"What about? Is it interesting?"

"Not so much so when I reread it years later, but it was the first American novel I read in middle school. It's about the car industry in Detroit."

"Oh," Mynah sounded disappointed, "Americans making cars. Not as if I can get one for myself." The next minute the languor in his tone changed to alert. "Wait, when was that, and how old were you then?"

Ou Hong ignored his probe.

"You came to our factory because of that book?" Liu Huagu asked, the dancing fire shadowing his face.

"Sort of," she said.

Liu Huagu said, "I'm listening."

"Me too," Mynah said languidly.

As Ou Hong began to tell her story, her voice changed little by little from cautious revelation to carefree retrospection.

5.

In 1972, because of her father's cooperative attitude, he was "liberated" by the Revolutionary Rebellion and "combined" into the "triumvirate" leadership, composed of representatives from the Rebellion, the military, and the repented old cadres. His cadre rank was reinstated at 13, which made Ou Hong a so-called "child of high ranking cadre," although she was really a border case. One privilege the high-ranking cadres had was the right to read "inside references." This was the way translated foreign books were labeled then. It was a restricted privilege, in that they could only read the books themselves and circulation was forbidden.

At that time, her father's bookshelves had been empty for a while, ever since the Red Guards raided their house. His favorites used to be the ancient works. One such was a thread-bare cloth bound book, with a blue cover and very delicate look, titled *Historical Mirrors for Rulers*, though she had no idea then what that meant.

("Me either," Mynah yawned. "It was hand-copied in delicate calligraphy; my father said it was the only-existing copy in the city," Ou Hong asserted. "An only-existing copy," Liu Huagu repeated in the dark. "Ahh, that'd be worth huge money now," Mynah commented.)

But it was gone with the house raid. Even after the Cultural Revolution, when most of the raided materials were returned to their family, there were no signs of that book. The loss of that book broke her father's heart; he hardly read books after that.

Because her father was a proponent of the quintessence of Chinese culture and wasn't interested in translations, the "inside references" issued him simply piled up on his bookshelf gathering dust. She was in middle school then, and she was often bored at school, where Party politics and propaganda were much more in evidence than science and literature. One evening she sneaked into her father's study and there was the translation of American writer Arthur Hailey's novel, *Wheels*, on its cover a black stamp: "For Criticism Only."

She took the book to her bedroom, closed the door, and read it into the night. She hadn't had a novel to read for several years and, with her hunger, any schlockered novel would have interested her. Yet this was a foreign novel, from America. The only translated novels she'd read before were from the Soviet Union: *Young Guards*, *Bravery*, etc.

Because she didn't finish it that night, the next morning she squeezed it into her book bag without telling her father. In the classroom, she put the book on her knees, covered it with a newspaper, and moved the newspaper along the line she was reading. She didn't think anyone would notice — all the students were chatting, kidding, throwing chalk to each other, and no one paid attention to the poor teacher.

She was wrong. The physics teacher noticed her slouching, something she never did in physics class, her favorite subject. Almost at the climax of the novel, the teacher asked her to answer a question. She heard her name being called and was startled, and she stood up in a flurry. The book, *Whump*, fell on the floor. The sound was like a thunder, and she was dumbfounded. The only thing she could think was, *My father is dead. Because of me.*

In the unusual quietness Master Liu walked to her. (Mynah turned to look at his master and Ou Hong said, "No, not him, of course.") This Master Liu was a member of the "Workers' Propaganda Team," or WPT, stationed in her school. This was the time for the "Working Class To Rule Everything," as Chairman Mao had ordained. The WPT members had absolute power on campus, and she had seen them scolding teachers and punishing students. This Master Liu was a quiet guy with a Buddha-like round face, but at that time she did not know what lay behind the façade.

Master Liu's steps sounded closer and closer. Her fear worsened. What would happen to her father when they found that a prohibited book had leaked from his hands? Would he be denounced again?

She stood still, desperately watching Master Liu approach. He picked up the book from the floor, nodded at her to sit down, and ordered the class to get back to the lesson.

That class period seemed to last forever. All the while her eyes were on Master Liu and his hands holding the book behind his back, as he strolled around students in the classroom. Wherever he stopped, the noise in that corner also stopped.

When the lesson finally ended and recess came, Ou Hong begged Master Liu to give her the book back. She pleaded that she would never misbehave again, and never read an irrelevant book in class again. Her hope was that, being only semi-literate, Master Liu would forgive her small transgression before he realized the novel was from an American imperialist.

Master Liu's face was taut. He told her he would think about it, and give her an answer in three days. She wondered what decision would take him three days to make, but she didn't dare to ask. And strangely, his timing gave her some comfort, like a delayed execution.

During those three days, each afternoon she returned from school worrying that her father would be denounced again. But no one seemed to notice the book's disappearance. On the third afternoon, she went to see Master Liu. He handed the book wrapped in newspaper back to her and said a bit apologetically, "There you are, kid. Thought to give my son the chance to read a foreign novel. He's a book lover. Now that he's finished, you can have it back."

"You didn't . . . I thought . . . " Ou Hong said incoherently, hugely relieved.

"*Shh*," he said, "don't bring it to school again, okay? It's dangerous."

"Did you read it too?" she asked.

"Nah, I can only recognize a handful of simplified characters. But my son told me about how Americans make cars. I wonder if we can have an automatic production line like theirs to make buses?"

"Which school is he in?"

"My son? He's older than you. An 'insert' in the countryside, just returned home for a short visit."

("Did the son like the book?" Mynah asked. "I was too relieved to ask Master Liu that. I just ran home and placed the book back on my father's shelf. I didn't even finish reading it." "He's a good master, as good as my master," Mynah said.)

By the time she was about to graduate from middle school, the movement of 'go help the development of border regions' had reached her city. This was similar to the earlier movement of "city youths go up the mountains and down to the countryside," except this time, it was aimed at kids aged 16 or above who were still in middle school. The campus boiled and the students were excited. Many petitioned to go to the remote Yunnan Province, to plant rubber trees and defend their country's southwest borders. Though Ou Hong was only 14, she also applied. When the long list of approved names that included almost everyone she knew was announced, her name wasn't on it. Was this a bad sign? Meaning she was not trustworthy? She ran to Master Liu to ask why.

"I took your name off the list, smart kid," Master Liu whispered to her, "we are now in the process of selecting one student from each class to go on to high school. Guess who I recommended for our class?"

Her pupils were dilated: "There will be a high school?"

"Yes," he said, "high schools will be reopened this fall, thanks to Premier Zhou Enlai."

So to high school she went. While her ex-classmates labored either in Yunnan's rubber-tree forest or in the countryside, she studied in a peaceful classroom. Unlike her middle school class, the students in her high school class were unfailingly industrious, knowing full well how miraculous their opportunity was. After that she never saw Master Liu again, and she hadn't even noticed when the Worker's Propaganda Team had disappeared from school. Not until years later, when she was about to graduate from university, had she realized what Master Liu had done for her.

6.

"Aha," Mynah said, "you came to look for that Master Liu!"

"You could say that."

"What's his name?"

"I'd never thought to ask his full name, I was just that stupid." Ou Hong let out a sigh.

"This surely makes things hard," Mynah said, "with no name. But he surely isn't my master. The age doesn't match."

"No, he could be the father of your master," Ou Hong said, and glanced at Liu Huagu, who didn't budge.

"My master's father passed away years ago," Mynah said. "What will you do if you find that Master Liu?"

"Thank him," she said simply.

They sat in silence for a moment. Then Ou Hong said to the listless Mynah, "Do you want to tell a story?"

"What kind do you like to hear?"

"Something about yourself, how about?"

"Myself. I'm hungry." Mynah took some bread out of his shoulder bag, bit it, and said with a mouthful, "You know the feeling of hunger?"

Liu Huagu said in a low voice, "Mynah, you don't have to tell it."

"Let me tell it tonight, Master. I was born in 1962," he paused at the number and checked Ou Hong's expression. "*They* say that was the end of the three-year famine. Not for my mother! My mom said she never once got enough to eat that whole year and she didn't have milk to nurse me. I was always crying with hunger. I lived, but I've got a stomach problem.

"Two years ago I failed the college entrance exam and didn't have a job. One weekend I drifted around on the street too long, until a little past noon. I forgot my mother's warning to return home on time. Suddenly I felt the hunger seizing me, and I was on the verge of losing consciousness. I ran to a nearby restaurant, to the nearest table, and opened my claw, yes, claw, at that moment my five fingers were not a hand, they were like an eagle claw. I thrust my claw into the first full rice bowl I found, grabbed a fist of hot rice and stuffed my mouth. I heard a woman screaming, before I knew I was under a waiter's crotch. His mother's! His fists fell on me like hailstones."

"Ouch," Ou Hong said.

"I shielded my head with my arms and kept chewing and swallowing. Then I stopped feeling the pain of the beating. I put down my arms and saw the waiter thrown aside by another man. The man looked at me, but didn't try to help me up. I saw from his eyes he wasn't sympathetic. 'Whatever you do would not be better than licking dishes?' He said this to me before going back to his lunch. I got on my feet and followed him to his table, where he sat with a nice woman. He frowned and pushed his bowl to me. I said 'No, I had enough, I want you to know I'm not a beggar.' I told him if I hadn't eaten a mouthful of food right away I would have passed out. Later I learned that the restaurant had a sign on its door, 'Beggars and Dogs not Allowed,' but I didn't see it then. Even if I had, I probably would have gone in anyway. The last thing I wanted was to lie on the street unconscious like a dead pig. I thanked him for helping me; then he told me his factory was recruiting new workers. I went there the following Monday. And here I am. My illness brought me a job paying a nice bonus."

"Who was . . ." Ou Hong began to ask. Liu Huagu threw a stick in the fire; the fire cracked and the sound submerged her words.

Mynah grinned cheekily, "As far as at the end of the sky, as close as in front of your eyes."

Liu Huagu cleared his throat and said, "Can I tell one?"

"Master," Mynah cried, "this is refreshing! I've never heard you tell a story!"

"Is it about yourself?" Ou Hong said.

Liu Huagu gave a slight nod.

"I'm listening," Ou Hong said.

"Before thirteen I was bellicose. ("Groovy," Mynah interrupted, while Liu Huagu subconsciously touched the corner skin of his slanted eye.) I had too much energy, and the schoolwork was easy for me. That was before the Cultural Revolution. Then at some point I was engrossed in reading novels based on true lives. One that mesmerized me was *Red Cliff*. ("Yeah, *Red Cliff*," Ou Hong nodded.) I imagined myself as a revolutionary jailed in the Sino-American Cooperation Camp on the Gele Mountains, being subjected to all kinds of cruel tortures but unwavering in the face of death. Of course in the end I wouldn't die like those in the book and reality. I would escape and go back to kill all the Nationalist agents. I felt life in peacetime was really boring, it didn't provide me any chance to become a hero.

"One day my school invited an old-generation revolutionary to give a speech. I was very surprised to learn that he had actually escaped from the Sino-American Cooperation Camp before its 1949 massacre. On his wrists remained the marks of ropes that once hung him from a beam. I was utterly touched. At the end of his speech he called to us, 'Love people, hate enemies! Be ready to become the successors to the revolutionary cause!' I could feel my blood bubbling at his calling, and the weight of historical duty falling on my shoulders. He changed me entirely. I became a 'three-good student' every semester, until the Cultural Revolution started. Imagine how shocked and angry I was to learn that this very revolutionary had become a capitalist roader . . ."

"Master, can you tell something more interesting?" Mynah interrupted, "we've all gone through those. The Cultural Revolution is really boring."

Liu Huagu left his story unfinished, despite Ou Hong's protest. When Mynah went to "refresh" in the woods, Ou Hong said to Liu Huagu quietly, "So you knew my father long ago."

"Not personally," he said. "Few in the city don't know about him."

"Is that why you have been taking care of me?"

"Not necessarily."

"So what is it?"

He said nothing but gazed at her, looking stern. For a prolonged moment two pairs of eyes locked on each other across the campfire, until Mynah returned.

Early the next morning, Liu Huagu woke Ou Hong, who had been soundly sleeping under two men's jackets. She lifted up the jackets and saw red embers still glowing in the campfire.

"Didn't you guys sleep at all?" She rubbed her eyes and asked.

Liu Huagu had already cleaned the chicken feathers and vegetable leaves out of the bus. He shouted with his back toward her, "You better get moving, the tow truck could be here any time." And, "Mynah, watch traffic for her."

Ou Hong remembered her mission and walked down into the ditch. She lay down behind the front wheels and squeezed her head and shoulders under the bus. She wasn't surprised to see the left wheel's rocker arm snapped. The question was, did it happen before the bus crash or after? Only a metallographic examination could tell.

She struggled out, still pondering, when her eyes met Mynah's staring at her shoulder. She looked down: dirt and grass tips dyed her snow-white shirt with brown and green. She grinned. Mynah and Liu Huagu both grinned. "Your smile looks real good," Mynah said. His comments made her wonder when was the last time she had smiled at men.

Later, on the way back, they saw a big sign "Here Often Causes Accidents." The road segment turned very narrow there; on their right was a deep valley, where the Jialing River roared. The sign was only 50 meters from where their bus had crashed.

7.

To Ou Hong, that night on the hill seemed to have formed a tacit understanding between the three of them, an invisible tie. Now Mynah's glib tongue made him cute, and Liu Huagu's glances from the corner of his wounded eye became a charming signature. She even thought about the possibility of staying in her job. She would be working in the Technical Division, she knew, and perhaps she could do something after all, like introducing modern technology into bus-making.

She didn't tell Liu Huagu and Mynah about the broken rocker arm. She didn't want to make them feel accused. It might have been a false alarm and she wanted a lab test first. Needless to say, there wasn't such a lab in the factory. But there was one in her university. In this Reform and Open Era, universities also wanted to make money. If her factory paid, the test could be done there.

She went to Manager Gao's office on the fourth floor of the Administration Building, and requested such a test. The fifty-ish man asked why and she stalled. It's unnecessary, he said, and if he had that money he'd rather pay it as a workers' bonus.

Before she tried to say more, a yelling came from downstairs: "Ou— Hong—"

She ran to the window. Downstairs in the open ground surrounded by office buildings and workshops, Yiping kneeled one leg down, holding a bouquet up, and shouted, "Ou Hong! If you don't come out today, I will not get up!" Apparently after his previous failures he had changed tactics. Soon his shouting brought people out from offices and shops, and the windows and doors were crammed with rubbernecking men and women in blue uniforms.

Ou Hong felt her face burning. This boy must have watched too many foreign movies! Making such a big scene! She ran down the stairs taking a devious path to the Chassis Shop, only to see that all the workers had gone to watch the dramatic scene, except Liu Huagu, who leaned on the wall and smoked, looking pensive. Seeing Ou Hong, his eyebrows barely rose.

"Help me," she said.

"You got a cute boy there," Liu Huagu said.

"I don't want him!"

"How interesting. Why not?"

She bit her lip and ran through the shop's front door to where Yiping was kneeling, still shouting her name. She pulled him up and said under her breath, "I hate men with soft knees!"

Yiping smiled and patted dust off his western trousers. He handed the bouquet to her with both hands: "For you."

Ou Hong did not take it. She said, "I already have a boyfriend."

"Don't fool me. Who? Where? You don't mean a worker in this place?" he laughed.

Ou Hong looked around and saw Liu Huagu now in the crowd at the Chassis Shop's gate watching them. She rushed into the crowd, grabbed Liu Huagu's hand, and dragged him to Yiping. She could feel Liu Huagu's hand first struggling in her grasp and then coming along.

"Him," she said to Yiping, not letting Liu Huagu's hand go. The crowd roared with laughter, some cheered, some whistled.

Yiping looked at the two standing in front of him, hands locked, both in blue overalls. He read the two faces back and forth, then froze to study Liu Huagu.

"I know who you are," Yiping said unexpectedly.

"I'm nobody," Liu Huagu said, his eyes meeting Yiping's challenge.

"I know who you are," Yiping repeated, laughing with the advantage. He whispered to Ou Hong, "Come home this weekend. I'll tell you who he is. You don't want to be with him." He threw the bouquet into her arm and left.

Ou Hong let out a nervous sigh and let go of Liu Huagu, who walked back to his people and ordered, "Show is over. Get back to work!"

That afternoon and the days following, the atmosphere was a bit strange in the Chassis Shop. Mynah was unusually quiet, and Liu Huagu hammered everything harder.

Then it was the May 1st International Labor Day, a long weekend. Ou Hong went home feeling lost. She told her father if Yiping knocked on the door, tell him she wasn't home. "I can't bear seeing him," she said. Her father's face, brightened by her return home, darkened a bit with her request, but she knew he'd do whatever made her happy.

Yiping didn't show up the first day. In the afternoon Ou Hong got a call. Her father answered the phone in his study and called out, "From your factory!" Her heart jumped, and she rushed to the phone, in time to wonder why his father's voice sounded so normal.

"*Wei*," she greeted softly to the receiver.

"Are you Ou Hong?" It was a woman's voice.

"Yes. Who are you?"

"I'm his wife."

"Whose?"

"Huagu's."

Ou Hong paused, trying to digest. "What can I do for you?" She said coldly.

"I, I just, please don't be mad at me . . ." the woman on the other end of the phone stammered, as if she was guilty. Ou Hong didn't know why she pictured a wrinkled yellow face, always obedient to her husband. She eased her tone of voice a little, "What do you want to tell me?"

"You, you have a bright future, endless possibilities. You don't have to have him . . ."

"Are you asking for my help to save your marriage?"

"No-no, I'm not talking about myself . . . you know, it's his future, his career I'm worried about . . . I know you have a good heart, please be kind, let him go. You know, a worker can make any mistake and still be fine, but a *male-female relationship problem* will destroy him. . . ."

Ou Hong began to feel annoyed. What was this woman, archaically calling an affair a "male-female relationship problem," doing? Was her pity begging a strategy? Ou Hong hadn't done anything, not yet!

"What did Liu Huagu tell you? Is he there? Let me speak to him!"

"No-no, he didn't tell me anything. He's not home. He went to Guan County this morning. . . ."

"Guan County?"

"Yes, he said he needs to find a bus part there," the wife's voice sounded relieved that now they were off the main topic, "he said it might take a couple of days."

"Did Manager Gao send him?"

"No-no, it's his own idea, told me not to tell anyone. But you are not an outsider," she now sounded flattering. "You won't tell him I called you, will you?"

"What is he looking for?"

"I don't know, something about an accident. . . ."

"In Guan County?"

"I don't know, oh, I've got to go, I'm using the factory's phone. Thanks for talking to me." *Click.* She hung up.

8.

The second day of the 3-day weekend, Ou Hong returned to the unfamiliarly quiet factory, hoping to find Mynah, who lived in the single-worker dorm. She found him drinking alone in the room he shared with two others. He offered Ou Hong a glass of white liquor and babbled with vertical eyes, "Miss University, I a . . . am not mad at you. I'd be really mad if it were not my master. My master is a good man, you are his match, his wife is not."

"Mynah, don't talk nonsense. You shouldn't drink this much, it will harm your stomach." She took away his liquor bottle and glass and made him hot tea. He obeyed her like a little boy.

"Tell me, did your master go to Guan County looking for a bus? Do you know why?" Ou Hong sat down with Mynah.

"He's gone? Didn't take me with him? After I told him I'm in? I said, 'Manager Gao doesn't give Miss University the rocker arm, we'll find another one for her!' "

"Mynah, I don't want just any rocker arm. . . ."

"I know, you want a broken one. I know. I'm not drunk."

Ou Hong finally figured out from Mynah's incoherent rambling that there was a bus accident in Guan County about half a year ago. It was a gruesome one. It was not in the newspaper because this kind of news had no benefit to our country's *stability and unity*. As the media and Manager Gao said everyday, we've had a decade of upheaval; now nothing goes before *stability and unity*.

However, rumors have legs. The news was so compelling that for quite a while it made the most relished chat over tea among the long-tongued women. It had happened on a small highway in Guan County. The bus suddenly veered across the centerline, in time for its side to be sheered off by a truck going the opposite direction. The entire side of the bus, the side with no passenger doors, was torn off like a piece of rotten cloth. A man's arm was severed at the shoulder joint, and a woman's mouth torn to her ear. Two were killed, and more were injured. The bus was made by their factory. How could it not have been? Theirs was the only bus factory in the city, and all the counties in the city's jurisdiction had to purchase buses from them. The investigation report concluded that it was the driver's fault, and the driver had died in the hospital. Afterward, Liu Huagu was sent to the county to see if the bus could be salvaged. It could not be, it was too badly damaged. He saw a fractured rocker arm then, but didn't think much of it until now.

9.

The third afternoon, Liu Huagu gave Ou Hong a pleasant surprise by showing up at her door, carrying one gift box in each hand. He politely greeted the father and the daughter, looking a bit timid, which was out of character.

"Let me guess what's in one of your boxes." Ou Hong said happily after introducing Liu Huagu to her father, "It's a rocker arm. Am I right?"

Liu Huagu sat there ill at ease. He gave her a single nod without a word.

"And the other one?" she asked.

"For Uncle," Liu Huagu said, there was vacillation in his voice, as if these two words were difficult to pronounce.

"You are too kind, Master Liu," Ou Hong's father said sincerely. "You are very welcome to be our guest. The working class is the leading class, eh? My daughter has a lot to learn from you."

An almost imperceptible frown brushed over Liu Huagu's eyebrows. Ou Hong rushed to cover for her father's bureaucratese: "May I open the gift for you, father?"

Rat-tat. Someone knocked at the door. The old man walked toward it.

"Don't open it, father!" Ou Hong cried. It was too late. Yiping stood at the open door. His glare passed Ou Hong and darted to Liu Huagu, who stood up. The two men, one inside and one outside, stared at each other as if swords were drawn and bows were bent.

"Uncle Ou," Yiping pointed to Liu Huagu, "he is—"

Liu Huagu interrupted him. "Uncle, the gift I brought for you is not really a gift. I am merely *returning the jade intact to the State of Zhao*," he alluded to an ancient adage.

The old man eyed the two young men with suspicion, and went to open the box. Ou Hong moved next to her father, and they both looked in.

An ancient book—covered in threadbare blue silk—lay in the box.

Ou Hong's father took it out carefully with both hands, trembling a little. He opened the book gently; inside the cover was a small square red seal with his own name in *Zhuan* style. He murmured, "What a gift, what a gift. Where did you find it, Master Liu? How can I thank you enough for this?"

Yiping stepped inside and said, "Uncle Ou, he led the raid of your house 16 years ago! I saw him!" His finger dramatically pointed to Liu Huagu. "He was a Red Guard leader in the Sixth Middle School then!"

The old man went still for a moment. He picked up his cane and asked, "Is that true?"

"Yes," Liu Huagu said.

"Yes! You have the face to say yes!" The old man suddenly exploded. "Look what you did to our country! To our culture!" He waved his cane to the empty bookshelves. "You destroyed everything, you Red Guards! History will never forgive you!"

With each of those accusing words, Liu Huagu's breath grew increasingly heavy, his vacillation giving way to indignation:

"So who taught us to destroy the Old World? Who taught us to hate the class enemies? Who taught us to be worthy successors of the revolutionary cause? You, you old cadres! The Party!"

Scenes from 16 years ago resurfaced; Ou Hong's eyes went dim. She broke up the men's heated exchange: "Can't you just apologize now?"

"No!" Her father and Liu Huagu shouted in unison.

She turned to Yiping, despairing.

"I will, I will," Yiping said eagerly. Then he asked her in an undertone, as if to convey a secret, "For what?"   #

WATCH THE THRILL

Spring and warmth have returned to our Iron Board Lane, but not the chirping sparrows, or the gurgling water that used to circulate around the rockery in Courtyard 9, my yard. Dwarf pine, holly willow, mosses, all the refined plants have withered away since the Cultural Revolution began. On dark nights the leafless grotesque dwarf trees can be unnerving, can be mistaken as naked ghosts; in bright daylight the desiccated brown sticks are just ugly.

Despite the rockery, my yard is a small one. It used to be called the "Directors' Yard." Only four families live in this yard, including my buddy Pipi's and mine. Boys like us spend most of our time in the next yard, Courtyard 14, because it's much larger, with ten-some households, and used to be really bustling. Don't ask me why numbers are missing between the two adjoining courtyards. I don't even know why people have gone missing.

After the bland lunch, Pipi and I loaf in the Lane, between the courtyards, as if something different from yesterday might happen. My grandma has asked me to take a noontime nap, but I told her no point, we have plenty of time to doze off in afternoon class.

Pipi fiddles with his slingshot and snaps empty shots into the sooty air. He can't find a target — no birds on roofs or power lines. The repeated *zing, zing* callouses my ear. Bathed in the blinding direct sun, the shadowless Lane is as quiet as a dead dog. Not just because it's noontime; the city's Police

Bureau is located right at the east end of our Lane.

"Let's wake everyone up," Pipi says. We are at the door of Courtyard 14.

He bellows a song of Chairman Mao's quotations at the top of his voice like a rednecked rooster:

"Revoluuuuutiooooon—"

The elated note that begins the unrhymed Quotation Song pumps me up right away and I join him, as rapid as firecrackers:

"Is not a dinner party,
or composing an essay,
or painting a picture,
or embroidering a flower.
It cannot be that refined,
that leisurely and gentle,
that temperate, kind, courteous,
restrained and magnanimous—"

In our indulgent bellowing we don't notice Wang Qiang approach. "Go howling for a damned funeral!" The teenager elbows us aside and reaches for the double-leaf wooden door. He carries a shoulder pole with two coal-blackened baskets. Black sweat streams down his oily bare shoulders.

The door swings open from inside, and there stands Uncle Yu, sleepy-eyed, mouth in the shape of a scolding word. But he swallows his word back at the sight of his teenage neighbor, and his facial muscles stiffen awkwardly. We stop singing, and scan the two faces. What is it they say? *The road is narrow for foes.* This has to be interesting.

Uncle Yu's face softens. "Had lunch yet?" He greets Wang Qiang.

We know Wang Qiang won't answer him. Wang Qiang would show the whites of his eyes. He might even spit on his older neighbor; he's been like that ever since his brother Wang Jian was sent away by Uncle Yu.

Except this time he disappoints us. As Uncle Yu makes way for him, he walks in with his throat making a mere bubbling sound that could almost be regarded as friendly.

The door swings shut. Uncle Yu has forgotten to scold us. Even if he remembered, he would have to stop as soon as he realized what we were singing. Just as the newspaper says every day — Chairman Mao's words are spiritual nuclear bombs with matchless power.

"What's wrong with Wang Qiang today?" I ask Pipi.

"I heard Uncle Yu's got a quota."

"What quota?"

"To bring the 'inserts' back, stupid."

"Really? Does Wang Jian have a chance?"

"Dunno." Pipi springs his slingshot again. "Something'll happen."

"In Iron Board Lane?" I'm not sure if his two comments are related.

Actually our Lane's name has been recently changed to "Destroy Capitalism Lane," but I am not used to that yet — a habit takes time to form. The Lane is sandwiched between two curves of high brick walls. Behind the wall on the north side are office buildings of the government agency, United Front Work Department, or UFWD, where my father used to be a director. Now he is a prisoner of the Revolutionary Rebellion (whose members were previously his subordinates). The wall on the south side surrounds our residential compounds, a chain of many courtyards. Facing the main entrance of UFWD is our Courtyard 9. The Lane is like a bow's arch connecting at both ends to Liberation Road, the bowstring.

At the west end of the bow, just meters from my yard, is the backdoor of the city's 2nd People's Hospital. The city's Police Bureau is located at the east end. The police have a yard many houses bigger than ours, with two policemen guarding its gate. Sometimes when a shining black car goes into the gate, the two handsome policemen "Pa!" stand at attention, and "Pa!" salute. (I try to imitate this, by stiffening, then swiftly raising my right hand to touch the brim of an imaginary service cap, but I just can't get it right.)

Needless to say Pipi and I are thrill watchers: where onlookers gather, you can count on finding us scurrying under the armpits of grownups, like two slippery loaches.

Fun things used to happen more often on the big street, like Red Guard demonstrations, faction fights, or truck parades exposing criminals and counterrevolutionaries, with arms tied high behind their backs and heavy name boards strapped around their necks. But lately the street has been quiet as well. The whole city has been quiet. There hasn't been much to watch. I think this is because all the young people—secondary school graduates like Wang Jian—have been "inserted" to the countryside. Like fallen leaves swept away by the autumn wind, they are gone. Without them the city is like an empty castle, kept only by the very young and the very old.

Once, the big thrill on the street was a bus accident. The bus driver first ran over a trash picker walking along one side of the road, then the driver must have panicked so badly he turned his bus across the street and onto the opposite sidewalk, grinding four more pedestrians. One person's head was cut off neatly from his neck, rolling on the road like a rubber ball. (Actually I didn't see the head; Pipi told me this.) I was a little late for that frightening fun because my grandma tried to block my way when I ran out. By the time I escaped her, the big street was already filled with a sea of people. Grownups are thrill watchers no less than we are. The bus was still there, half straddling the sidewalk, but the driver and the bodies were gone. Pipi pointed out several bloodstains on the ground to me, but they looked more like oily dirt than blood. I was disappointed.

This kind of thrill doesn't happen often. Days are usually boring, no parents at home (only a grandma), no real school to go to (my elementary class reads nothing but the editorials of the *People's Daily* newspaper and the *Red Flag* magazine), no books to read (all either burned or seized). It's strange how such a complete freedom turns to boredom. No movies to watch either. Actually that isn't totally true. In the whole of China, three warfare movies have been playing in cinemas all these years: *The Mine Warfare*, *The Tunnel Warfare*, and *The Warfare on the Plain*. I liked the movies, but after repeatedly watching them I can recite almost every line, be it a Japanese devil's or a guerrilla hero's. We eight hundred million Chinese also get to watch eight model revolutionary Beijing Operas, directed by Chairman Mao's wife. With all these we shouldn't be feeling so bored, I suppose, but the truth is, we are.

"I'll give you anything if you find me fun to watch," I say to Pipi.

He replies, "I'll give you my slingshot if you let me share your meat ration."

I know his hungry tummy has already consumed his half-pound meat ration this month, because my grandma cooked it for him. He is 12, almost a year older than me, and you can always find in his dusty pockets a handful of thumb-size pebbles. These are the "bullets" for his slingshot. It was a farewell gift from Wang Jian, a middle school graduate in Courtyard 14, before he was inserted to the countryside for re-education by poor peasants. Pipi used to shoot sparrows with the slingshot, that is, when there were still sparrows to shoot. There were good days, such as when Pipi took the wounded or dead birds to my house and asked my grandma to cook a stew. We called our sparrow stew "communism," a joke about the Soviet Union revisionist Kruschev's "communism = potato + beef stew" that we were criticizing in school. I'm more hungry for fun; I would have exchanged my meat ration for his slingshot if there were still sparrows around. Now that we haven't seen any birds for a long time, he is as bored as I am, even with his slingshot.

I wonder why Wang Jian didn't give me the slingshot, was it because he thought I was not as brave a boy as Pipi? Like Pipi, I used to hang out with the Wang brothers a lot. The door of their house was always open, and if you went in you'd often get a treat — like a handful of sand-fried broad beans or something — from Mother Wang. I think I know why Mother Wang gave her sons such names. "Jian" means "healthy" and "Qiang" means "strong." She must have wished her sons would not be as sickly as their father, who died years ago of chronic TB. Her wish came true in Wang Qiang, the muscled, stocky younger brother, while in contrast Wang Jian was a pale-skinned, trim young man wearing thick glasses. "Bookworm," old Mother Wang would say, praising and cursing her son in one affable breath. She is a housewife whose heart and eyes are only on her sons, and she has no idea what's going on in the world. "What book is he reading?" I once asked her. "Child, are you asking me? I'm an open-eye blind," the old lady answered, mending the elbow of a boy's shirt, "if you show me the number 'one,' I can tell you it's a shoulder pole." "You are illiterate!" I exclaimed. "Well, I can recite 'Five Word Canon,' can you?" she said. I'd never heard such a thing so I urged her to recite it. She chanted in her aged singsong voice:

> "At birth, man is kind,
> Then growth, sets the mind.
> Cultivation, to keep man's nature;
> Chiseling, to shape the treasure . . ."

Despite the melodious rhythms, her chanting sounded alien and non-revolutionary. "That's feudal residue!" I interrupted, regurgitating commonplace words from the newspaper. The old lady stopped chanting and mending, staring at me with her illiterate stare. "It's a children's song from when I was your age," she said at last. "That was a feudal time," I pointed out to her, "class enemies aren't born kind!" But she could make no sense of what I said.

It was Wang Jian the bookworm who had been a magnet to us. On hot summer nights, a crowd of us brought stools or bamboo mats to the front of the Wang family's door, in Courtyard 14, to listen to Wang Jian's ghost stories. He sat on a bench, and waved a feather fan like Zhuge Liang the ancient war strategist. His weird ghost stories scared the piss out of us; the chills in our spine cooled the August out of our skins.

Wang Qiang sat by his brother and toyed with a flashlight when Wang Jian told his story. "Once upon a time there was a compound, and its latrine was half a mile away. One night a boy like you —" he pointed to me with his feather fan, "— needed to go badly. On the way to the latrine he saw a man in front walking with a lantern. As he ran past the man the boy threw him a glance. The boy got into the latrine and squatted over a pit. There was another man squatting over the next pit, and the latrine was quite dark. The boy couldn't help but say, 'Did you see that man with a lantern? Something is not right about him.' 'What's wrong with that man with a lantern?' The other man asked in the dark. 'His face is too long,' the boy said."

At this point Wang Jian pointed somewhere behind us with his fan, and we all turned to look where he pointed. There was a cold tingling sensation at the nape of my neck as Wang Jian's bewitching voice continued. " 'Look at me,' the man squatting next to the boy said and raised a lantern, 'isn't my face long too?' "

We instantly turned back, and all screamed. A ghost face! Wang Qiang had turned on his flashlight and held it right below his chin. The narrow ray of light shot upward through his nose, highlighting a pair of eye-whites and a long, red tongue sticking out like that of a strangled man, and shadowing the rest of his face. Enjoying our horrified reaction, Wang Qiang dropped the flashlight and laughed like a squawking duck. His elder brother, the storyteller, did not even leak a smile.

"Want another one?" Wang Jian always asked after we calmed down. "Yes! Yes!" We replied invariably. There are things like that, the more scared you get, the more you want them. Unfortunately, there is no banquet that does not disperse. Wang Jian had to go to the countryside; since then Courtyard 14 has been deserted.

The younger brother, Wang Qiang, is a much quieter guy. I guess this is because he has a slight stutter; it becomes obvious only when he is upset. To say I liked him is less true than that I liked his wolfhound. That was before the city banned dogs. The dog was another thing that frightened me and attracted me at the same time. One day I saw Wang Qiang walking his dog in our Lane. I ran home and cut a piece of raw pork from my mother's grocery basket. That was when my mother was still home and the grocery stores still had meat on their shelves. I thought I would please the dog, and Wang Qiang, with the pork. Sure enough, as soon as the dog smelled the pork it groaned excitedly and its eyes glowed red. It lunged toward me, pulling the leash so taut that Wang Qiang almost lost his grip on it. I retracted a step in fear. Wang Qiang dragged the dog to his side and, boy, how upset he got! "What are you d-d-doing, you s-s-stupid boy?" He yelled. "Never let a dog t-t-taste raw blood! Understand?" The truth is I didn't. I still don't understand why my good will had put him in such a temper. Later, the wolfhound was killed by the police "Dog Destroying Team," and Wang Qiang cried like a baby. When he stopped crying, his eyes were shining red. I wondered if his beloved dog had given him those eyes.

I wish it were Wang Qiang who went to the country instead of his elder brother. Uncle Yu, whose job was to mobilize unwilling young people to go to the countryside, had given the Wang family a choice. "One of your two sons must go," Uncle Yu told Mother Wang, "your family can decide which one." The problem was that Wang Jian and Wang Qiang are the tightest brothers I've ever seen. They never fought or argued like brothers in other families. They quarreled hard for the first time over who should go. Wang Jian said he was older and it was his duty; Wang Qiang said he was stronger and would more likely survive the hard labor. Their mother just kept sighing like bellows. In the end Wang Jian won. Since then Wang Qiang has not hidden his animosity toward Uncle Yu.

I like Uncle Yu. He is an amiable man in his fifties. Back when I was still in kindergarten, and my parents were still busy at work, Uncle Yu used to pick me up and carry me home every afternoon. He did that for years. When my father thanked him, he waved both palms like fans and said, "It's nothing, it's nothing." He was a medium-sized guy, but when he let me ride on his shoulders, I felt like I was high up in the clouds. Even after my father got denounced, and he criticized my father as hard as others, he was still nice to me. Once I asked him why he was so mean to my father, he looked surprised. "It's revolution, kiddo, not personal," he said, "your father is a capitalist roader. He's our class enemy now. You must draw a clear line between you and him!" I wondered how I would do that when my father comes home. That is, if he does come back. It's not as if I could use a chalk on the living room floor.

Wang Jian the "insert" came home for a short visit once. He looked emaciated. His face and arms were sun-darkened, and he had acquired a few strands of white hair, like a little old man. We call that kind of hair "juvenile white." Maybe one in a hundred boys get that kind of hair. I didn't think he had it before. Maybe he worries too much in the countryside. Worry can whiten one's hair, I heard. But his personality change was even more apparent than his physical change. He became so quiet, even quieter than his younger brother. I asked him if the countryside was fun. He didn't answer at first. When I asked again, he said, "Not when you don't know if you will ever get your city registration back." His tone made me fear that one day his fate would be mine, too.

⁓

Uncle Yu must have done a great job to mobilize the middle school graduates, because he is promoted to head the "Youth Placement Office." From the gate of my yard I can see the two big windows of his office on the second floor of the main office building. As far as I can tell, this is the only office in UFWD that has any function. In all other offices, the grownups take turns reading the newspaper aloud, oblivious of what their audience does. Usually they are chatting or dozing off; I think they are as bored as I am, they just don't admit it. But Uncle Yu is actually quite busy. Recently his office is packed with parents who have children "inserted" to the countryside.

These days Wang Qiang goes in Uncle Yu's office frequently. When he gets out his face is a barometer, changing between sunny, cloudy and thunder-stormy. It must be very hard for him to beg his opponent each time. I wonder if he will get his brother back, and if he does, will we get to hear ghost stories again?

"Wang Jian has no hope," Pipi says to me after spying on Uncle Yu's office and house several times.

"How do you know?"

"Look at the people who see Uncle Yu often: Auntie Zhang works in the meat counter of the grocery store. Grandpa Xu's nephew is an official in the city's Revolutionary Committee. What can the Wang family give to Uncle Yu? They don't have money. They don't have anything."

"Uncle Yu is not like that," I say, "he's a good guy."

"Hearts are separated by belly skins," Pipi says old-mannishly, "you never know what they really are. But if Uncle Yu really doesn't take anything from anyone, then that's even worse for the Wang family."

I think Pipi is right. It is hard to imagine how Wang Qiang, with his stutter and hard-to-conceal animosity, could convince Uncle Yu to place Wang Jian's name on the top of the list. After all, over a hundred kids of UFWD employees are toiling in the countryside, and the quota Uncle Yu has is merely four.

It comes as no surprise to us that Wang Jian is not among the "inserts" who are chosen to return home.

This afternoon Pipi and I are hanging out at our gate, staring at the quiet Lane, bored. The only vaguely interesting thing that happened was when Wang Qiang walked into the UFWD gate earlier. It is summer again and our city is like an oven, but he wore a long sleeve shirt, with neat, gray patches sewn on the elbows. His hands were in his pant pockets and he did not even look at us. We knew he was going to Uncle Yu's office, and we expected to hear arguing.

The quarrelling voices poured out of Uncle Yu's office window: just what we were waiting for. But something is unusual today. We hear tables and chairs being knocked down, heavy footsteps stamping rapidly on the wooden floor. Then screams. Screams and shouting. We are frozen.

Wang Qiang appears at the UFWD gate, panting. His eyes are as red as his wolfhound's. A dagger is in his right hand, dripping blood. Real red blood! The old doorman hurriedly steps aside. Wang Qiang pauses at the door, as if to decide which direction to run. He should run to the west end, I think, not only because it is shorter to the Liberation Road, but it is also away from the police. To my surprise, he runs east, toward the Police Bureau!

Before we recover from our shock, Uncle Yu comes after him. Uncle Yu's white shirt is soaked in blood and he is staggering. His screaming is as shrill as crows crying in a graveyard. The screaming brings people out from every office and courtyard. Unlike Uncle Yu, however, the crowd is cautious; it keeps a certain distance when following Wang Qiang. Now excitement takes us over. Pipi and I jump into the crowd.

On the concrete pavement, Wang Qiang runs like a madman. When he gets closer to the police gate, he drops his dagger. As soon as this happens, the following crowd yells out and chases him as madly as he runs. People shout: "Catch him!" We echo: "Catch him!" All the while Uncle Yu runs in front; blood streaming from his body: head, shoulders, arms, back. I can't see his front, but am pretty sure there is also blood running down his chest.

And he catches Wang Qiang! He grabs a corner of Wang Qiang's shirt that flows behind. But Wang Qiang strips off the shirt and keeps running. Uncle Yu falls on the ground, clutching the shirt. He tries to get on his feet again but fails. Some adults hurry over to him and shout about taking him to the hospital. I have a second of hesitation: should I follow the chase, or follow those to the hospital? Either way I will have plenty to watch, but they are in different directions. I have never faced such a directional choice before.

Pipi and the majority of the crowd show no hesitation. Someone is yelling: "He's going in the Police Bureau! Don't let him!" I see that Wang Qiang has only a short distance from the police gate. The police guards have already pulled their pistols out and aimed at him. I'm puzzled: why don't people let Wang Qiang run to the police? Isn't it easier to arrest him there?

I hear Wang Qiang's ducky voice, "D-d-don't shoot, officer! Let me in! I c-c-come to give myself up!" His steps slow down, and he raises two empty hands above his bare shoulders. One of the policemen lowers his pistol.

At this moment, *zing*! A pebble races at Wang Qiang and hits his leg. The leg bends, and he falls down. People rush up and pin him on the ground; the policemen pull their pistols back and calmly watch. People truss Wang Qiang up so tight like tying a pyramid-shaped sweet rice dumpling. To my surprise, he does not make a single groan.

He is only one step short of the Police Bureau's gate.

"You didn't have to use your slingshot. He had no way to escape." I say to Pipi after all the frenzy has passed and people have handed the tied-up Wang Qiang over to the police. I can't hide my envy.

"Didn't you hear? We can't let the murderer get in the Police Bureau!"

"Why not? The police will catch him."

"You silly, don't you know the Party's policy, 'Be lenient to those who confess; be severe to those who resist'? If he gets in there, it is called a surrender, then he won't get the death penalty."

"He will now?"

"For sure. It's my credit! They should reward me." Pipi looks so proud and satisfied. I guess he has the right to be. If his parents hadn't gone missing they too would be helped by his glory.

Uncle Yu died in the hospital that day. And Pipi's prediction about Wang Qiang comes true. In a few months flyers of sentenced criminals are all over our walls. The photo of Wang Qiang, with a red X on it to indicate death penalty, looks unfamiliar, hair shaved and eyes numb and all that. "His crime has roused the greatest public indignation that can only be pacified by his capital punishment," the flyer reads.

For all the time after Wang Qiang was jailed, we didn't hear anything from Wang Jian. I don't know if he is too ashamed to visit home. Sometimes I would remember those days we sat with the Wang brothers and listened to their ghost stories with frightened hearts. But I know I shouldn't have any sympathy for Wang Qiang. He is a bad guy now. If one kills a good guy, then he is a bad guy. Uncle Yu was a good guy; everyone says that.

The public execution will take place tomorrow, in the Da Tianwan Stadium, immediately after the public trial. It is the biggest thrill ever. All of my playmates and I plan to go watch it. And we have to get up early in order to occupy good spots in the front, so that we won't miss a thing. Pipi, and everyone, is excited. Whatever uneasiness I had is drowned by their enthusiasm. I have only seen executions in movies before. We want to see what Wang Qiang's expression is like when he's being shot. And, after that, we will have something to chat about for days, even weeks, and life will be less boring for a while.

The only thing casting a little shadow on my excitement is Mother Wang. Since Wang Qiang killed Uncle Yu, whenever I go to Courtyard 14, I can't help peeping at the Wang family's door or window, now always tightly shut. Today Mother Wang sees me. The white-haired old lady stares at me with two sunken eyes, so black, like two bottomless holes, they scare my guts out. I wonder if she has gone mad. #

DISCIPLE OF THE MASSES

Winter

Shanzi marched to the cadence of deafening gongs and drums beneath red flags snapping in the north wind. With her fellow high school graduates, she descended the stone steps into the Heaven Gate Port. Winter plum was in full bloom on the riverside hills; its waxy blossoms perfumed the chilly February morning, as if to celebrate her expedition. Boarding The East is Red, she saw her parents waving in the square at the top of the steps. The tears she knew were in her mother's eyes tinged her jubilant mood with guilt, and she scampered into the ship's cabin without looking back.

Soon the ship left all behind: the winter plum on the wind, the familiar port with the long flight of stone steps, her high school and her favorite math teacher. Parents receded into black dots as the ship chugged down the Yangtze River. Somewhere a girl began to sob, a boy whistled a melancholic Russian song. Someone yelled, Stop, and quartets formed to play cards.

Alone in a corner, Shanzi sat cross-legged on the ship's dirty floor, half-smiling at a piece of lined paper in her hand: Mr. Tan's neat set of equalities: *Goldbach's Conjecture.*

For an instance she saw Mr. Tan's nearsighted gaze behind glasses. A delicate blue china vase with winter plum bouquet. A calculus book opened on the desk. He was asking, "Do you know why you're being sent to the countryside?" A strange question, considering the mandatory transfer of secondary school graduates into the mountains and countryside that had been carried out for years.

The smile lapsed from Shanzi's face as she remembered her math teacher, sitting beside the vase, one fist pressed against his forehead, exposing blue veins on both his forehead and hand. She had never seen him so sad. His face mottled with an unfathomable shadow when he asked, "Do you know the famous problem '1+1'?"

"I know 1+1=2." Shanzi chuckled.

Mr. Tan wrote down something on a piece of paper and handed to her:

12 = 5+7
40 = 3+37
100 = 41+59

"What pattern do you see here, classmate Shanzi?" he prompted as if they were in class.

"I'm not a 'classmate' anymore," she mumbled, then exclaimed: "Neat! On the left hand we have all even numbers; on the right, the sum of two primes."

He nodded. "Looks simple, doesn't it? That any even number can be expressed as the sum of two primes. It's called Goldbach's Conjecture, the problem of 1+1. For almost a century no one has been able to prove it."

Aha. One prime plus one prime. The numbers intrigued Shanzi, as numbers always did. For a while she couldn't take her eyes away from those neatly written equalities. She ran off bigger numbers in her head, and the conjecture held true. So simple, yet she had no clue how to start a proof.

Mr. Tan had said, "It once was my dream to solve this, but the hope is on you now." With a sigh he gave her the calculus book that he had been teaching her behind the Revolution Committee's censoring. The sweetness of winter plum scented a moment of quietness. She asked him then, "Do you have any advice for me?"

"Live gingerly. Think three times before speaking. Em?"

On the third afternoon the "inserts" arrived at a desolate rural port. A dilapidated long-distance bus picked them up. Two hours later, their bumpy ride ended in a dirt field at the edge of a single-street town. A group of peasants in dark-colored, homemade cotton jackets waited silently, bamboo pipes in their teeth, arms folded, necks pulled into collars. Dirty-faced preschool boys gawked from nearby. Beyond them lay the Commune of New Wonders.

Shanzi's excitement waned. The waiting peasants' wooden faces showed no emotion, reminding her of a wartime photo from the 1930s, in which expressionless Chinese onlookers crowd around a Japanese soldier beheading a Chinese man. With deep grief, Lu Xun, the great writer of the '30s, had called his fellow Chinese *my sleeping people*. To Shanzi, those onlookers had been numbed by too many deaths during the Japanese invasion. But what numbed people here, now?

At the bus door, Secretary Xia, the number one leader of the commune, appeared in a fur-collared army coat and shook hands with each city insert. "Welcome, welcome," he repeated in local dialect. A handsome man in his mid-thirties, he had a clean-shaven face in contrast to the peasants and the newspaper image of sun-darkened, hard-working country cadres. He appeared to Shanzi as one who had never worked in the fields.

While the winter sky faded to gray, the peasants took away one after another of the city youths. The dirt field emptied, but no one came for Shanzi. She sat on one of her camphorwood suitcases, next to her quilt pack, and waited.

Secretary Xia approached, accompanied by a younger man, and asked her name, age, and home city. Then he told her, "They'll be here. Don't worry. Who'd have eaten a leopard's gallbladder to disobey Chairman Mao's instructions, huh?" He laughed.

Shanzi grinned, thankful for company. Across the bus road, an empty trail zigzagged into undulating hills where, somewhere, there was a Lily Village that would become her new home. A moment later, an announcement blared from a loudspeaker on an electricity pole in a corner of the field: *Sixth production team of Lily Village, sixth production team of Lily Village: please hurry to receive your insert, please hurry to receive your insert.* She looked at the fields, the street, the few low buildings, trying to find something familiar.

An evening fog fell, blending with the smoke from chimneys. Her stomach rumbled. This had never happened once in her 17 years of life: she did not know where to find her supper.

"Here they are!" shouted the tall young man standing beside Secretary Xia; he had been so quiet she had scarcely noticed him. He sounded even more relieved than she felt, and she smiled at him. He smiled back, the long narrow eyes on his bookish face curving into new moons.

Two people emerged from the fog: a middle-aged peasant and a girl Shanzi's age, each carrying a shoulder-pole. The girl also had an empty bamboo basket hooked on her back. Secretary Xia thundered, "Head Chen, you seem to have a habit of being late!" The Secretary surprised Shanzi, scolding an older man. She covered her mouth to push back a nervous titter, and the older man hemmed and hawed in village dialect.

The girl, dressed in a floral jacket and a bit shorter than Shanzi, resembled a cotton flower bud. She weighed one of Shanzi's suitcases in her hand. "Oyee! Did you put bricks in it?"

Shanzi stood up, relieved, "I brought lots of books about scientific agriculture."

"Books are no different from bricks to me. I'm Zhou Zhifen. All call me Zhou Sixth."

"Sixth? You have five siblings?"

"What? I have an older brother, and a younger brother called Zhou Eighth."

The answer chilled Shanzi. So five of Zhou Sixth's siblings had died? Zhou Sixth handed her shoulder-pole to Shanzi and bent over to place the quilt pack in her back-basket. "Hey," she said. "What's that?"

"My flute."

"Can you blow it?"

"Later. If you have bamboo, we can make a flute for you too."

"Really? We have no shortage of bamboo." Zhou Sixth was quick. "Head!" She shouted at the older man, "the wood boxes are yours!" But he was still being scolded by Secretary Xia. "Come on," Zhou Sixth said to Shanzi.

Shanzi hesitated: "The suitcases are heavy. . . ."

"Head's got iron shoulders. Besides, what can your stringy arms carry?" Her ringing laughter opened Shanzi's heart and, carrying the empty shoulder-pole, she tried to keep up. Zhou Sixth said they had been late because Head Chen had to break up a fight between a pair of newlyweds, Jinling and Chen Ying. The fight was about their baby.

"What's wrong with it?"

"It's a girl."

"That's old thought," said Shanzi. "Chairman Mao said women can hold up half the sky!"

"That's in your city. In our place a girl is just a dowry-debt."

Head Chen overtook them, shoulder-pole bowed from the suitcases on each end. He was not even breathing heavily. Shanzi felt an urge to thank him, but was frightened by his sulky, wrinkled face; she was no longer sure if she really had seen an obedient expression on this face earlier.

"What's up, Head?" Zhou Sixth asked.

"Secretary Xia ordered a re-survey of our rice fields."

This silenced Zhou Sixth. Shanzi almost spoke, but she remembered Mr. Tan's advice: *think three times before speaking.* Instead she asked, "Where are the winter plum trees?"

"Winter plum? Ah!" Zhou Sixth said. "I remember seeing those flowers when I was a bare-buttock kid. All cut down, long ago in the Great Leap Forward."

"All cut? Winter plum?"

Zhou Sixth threw her a disapproving glance. "What's the fuss? Can flowers fill your belly?"

Shanzi fell silent. For the rest of the half-hour walk to Lily Village, no one spoke.

Early next morning Shanzi woke to booming music —"The East Is Red"— from a loudspeaker on her wall. She groped for a string between her bed and the overhead light before remembering the adobe house had no electricity. The wooden shutters let in no light, but it had to be 6:00am, the time the radio station started the familiar music. Along with the anthem, dogs were barking, chickens cackling, pigs grunting, and neighbors walking in the courtyard.

She jumped out of her warm quilt, quickly dressed, walked out of her new bedroom into a small space piled with straw from last year's rice plants, and opened the courtyard door. Cold wind sent shivers down her spine, even with her thick jacket on. In the glimmering of dawn, she saw frost-whitened roofs and the courtyard.

Then she stilled.

Just outside her doorsill, a motionless brown chicken stood with one foot on the ground, the other drawn up under its wing. Its black eyes stared at her like dull pearls. After a few seconds, she probed it with a finger. Frozen. It dropped like a rock.

Shanzi screamed and Auntie Chen, Head Chen's wife, ran in with their youngest child, a five-year-old girl. The barefoot child got there first and stared at the chicken, with the same expression she had last night, when Auntie Chen gave Shanzi a bowl of steamy noodles. Shanzi had been too hungry to wonder why she ate alone. She had never known plain noodles — with just a pinch of salt and chopped chili peppers, no oil, not even soy sauce — could be so tasty. She had slurped noisily when Auntie Chen roared in, grabbed up the little girl from a dark nook, and struck the child's palm with chopsticks: "You unworth! Never seen anyone eat?" The little girl broke free and ran away, after giving Shanzi a dismal look.

Seeing the frozen chicken, Auntie Chen clapped her hands and fell on Shanzi's doorsill. "Oh heavens, my heavens, don't you want us to live? My last handful of noodles fed to the insert, now my last hen gone, no more eggs, oh ho ho . . ." No one could stop her from crying.

Zhou Sixth, clicking her tongue, arrived from the neighboring courtyard and walked into Shanzi's faggot room. She pointed to the broken bricks stacked in front of a dish-sized hole in the outer wall: "You did that?"

"Yes. I was stopping the wind . . ." Shanzi's new home had been a grain storage shed, unused for a long time. Months before, under the commune's supervision, villagers had added an inside wall to give the insert assigned to them a faggot space, like any proper farm house. Shanzi, who had never spent a night outside the city, didn't know a sitting hen had made its nest in her faggot room, the hole in the wall its doorway. Or that her first night would be the coldest.

Head Chen returned, and his wife's loud cries subsided. He saw the chicken and muttered a curse, then yelled at his wife to get back home and cook the chicken. The little girl's dirty face brightened as she ran after her mother. Awaking from her shame, Shanzi caught up with Head Chen and handed him a two-yuan bill, a month's stipend from her mother, enough to buy a young chicken.

Head Chen pushed her hand away and said without a smile: "I have one more bowl of gruel for you this morning. You must cook your own lunch today."

"I want to help! Let me help!"

He paused. "Help? It's enough if you don't make more trouble." He stepped over his high doorsill and disappeared.

Shanzi stared at his open door. Zhou Sixth whispered to her, "Head's not a bad guy, he just talks that way. You'll learn. I'll help."

Shanzi felt someone else nearby. She turned to see a pretty woman in her early twenties standing at the door on the left, an infant sleeping on her back. Watching Shanzi, the woman's egg-shaped face had an unreadable expression; perhaps a smile, perhaps not. Shanzi guessed it was the newlywed, Chen Ying, but couldn't read the woman's reaction — just as last night she couldn't read the eyes of the five-year-old girl. She wished someone could interpret these faces for her.

Later, unpacking her suitcases, she sought out the little red book *Chairman Mao's Quotations,* and flipped through its pages. *Be the disciple of the masses first, then the sensei of them,* she read.

Spring

February coldness disappeared overnight, and March came with blossoms of peach, plum, and apricot. In the seedbeds, dense rice seedlings started to green, soon to be transplanted into the hundreds of water-filled paddy fields around the village. Cuckoos flew over houses and hills calling *Boo-Goo! Boo-Goo! — Plant rice! Plant rice!* Men waded in thigh-deep mud, both hands holding the wooden plows pulled by water buffalo. From time to time a whip cracked over a water buffalo's horns.

Shanzi had only seen peach blossoms in static paintings. She marveled at the massive pink clouds unfolding over the earthen ridges that divided the fields. The scentless petals — smooth as water, rioting colors of fire — wafted onto her hair, shoulders, open palms. In her heart, a string plucked

— Itching? Longing? Distress?

The first time she picked a branch of peach blossoms, Head Chen scowled. "That's a few less peaches to sell." Though embarrassed at being caught, she could not stop. She kept doing it behind the villagers' backs.

If Shanzi reveled in Lily Village's spring landscape, she was enamored higher up on the mountains another day, when she went with Zhou Sixth to collect firewood.

Over the past weeks, Shanzi had learned — thanks to Zhou Sixth — to pull up a full bucket of water from a deep well and to carry a pair of water buckets on a shoulder-pole without spilling much. Now she could make a good fire in her new kitchen range, built in the faggot space. Eventually she cooked a wok of rice that wasn't burnt or undercooked.

The initial firewood allotted her by Head Chen — a small bundle from each of the nineteen families in the four courtyards — never materialized. She got ten bundles, and Chen Ying, her left-door, newlywed neighbor, made a long face when handing over her bundle under Head Chen's scrutiny. Head Chen asked if Shanzi had gotten everything and, face burning, she said *yes*. He nodded, appearing satisfied.

In a few weeks her firewood ran out. For the first time in her life, she faced a real danger of going hungry.

"How can you burn nineteen bundles so quickly? " Zhou Sixth asked. Shanzi's eyes brimmed with tears. "Okay, okay," Zhou Sixth comforted. "Don't be this way. You'll have firewood but no rice, or rice but no firewood." She yelled at Head Chen, "Head! Are you going to starve the insert?" That got her permission to take Shanzi to the higher mountains while earning work points.

Except for Zhou Sixth's family, most villagers kept their distance from the city girl. And something baffled Shanzi further: during teamwork, people moved languidly, but at the hammering of the off-work gong they ran from the collective land to their own family plots where they immediately turned into dynamos. These were not the poor peasants that Chairman Mao wanted the city youths to learn from. Besides, each peasant was allowed only a tenth of a *mu* of land for private use, not enough for planting grain. Since they had to rely on the collective land for the big chunk of their own food, not to mention needing to make a contribution to their country, why didn't they work harder?

On the mountains, Shanzi asked Zhou Sixth why the villagers seemed to dislike her.

"Because you get rice ration from the government, I guess."

"That's only for my first year. You think they'll be nicer to me next year?"

"Hard to say. Maybe they will, if they see you're not on the commune's side."

"But isn't the commune our own government?" Shanzi debated, to which Zhou Sixth shrugged, "I don't know. Don't talk big lines to me. Lines don't substitute for rice."

"Why are you so nice to me then?"

Zhou Sixth paused. "Maybe because my elder brother also eats public rice? He's in the army. Or maybe because you are prettier than me." She laughed, dodging Shanzi as she tried to tickle her armpits. Their laughter frightened a flock of sparrows out of a maple, and Shanzi's eyes followed the flapping wings. Holding the maple tree, she looked down, and saw it: A small village lay in the valley, surrounded by a peach orchard. Several thatch houses scattered in graceful disorder inside the ring of pink clouds. Lush vegetables grew in tidy rows; ducklings circled their enclosure; light blue smoke rose from chimneys into the sunny sky.

Shanzi whispered, "What a . . . *utopia*."

"What a *what*?" Zhou Sixth asked.

"Oh, other-worldly place." Shanzi pointed to the village, "Don't you want to live there?"

"*Ha ha ha ha!*" Zhou Sixth laughed so hard that she bent over and held her stomach. When she managed to halt the laughter she said: "No, I don't. It's a leper village."

"*L . . . Leper village!*" Horrible images of faces and hands with rotten, decomposed skin appeared to Shanzi, so vivid that she averted her eyes, as if one more look at that beautiful village would bring deadly contagion to her.

"How do people live there?"

"Plant and eat, get full." Zhou Sixth said, not without envy. "They don't pay public grain, but they can't leave the village. The government drops them medicine and salt every month."

Shanzi found this so hard to believe: the most beautiful place she had ever seen turned out to be the sickliest. On the return trip from the high mountains, under the pressure of the faggot bundles heaped on her shoulders, she forgot about the utopia.

After Shanzi's arrival, a new sound joined Lily Village's morning chorus of barks, cackles, and oinks. She often practiced her flute at dawn, before the day exhausted her. Sometimes sporadic off-key notes from the next courtyard echoed her melody — Shanzi had helped Zhou Sixth to make a bamboo flute by hand. Although the eight holes of the new flute were burned with a fire poker and the second hole was covered with rough bamboo membrane, its sounds were nice enough to please Zhou Sixth and her younger brother. Shanzi congratulated herself on making her first product in life.

The music did not make everyone happy. "Who's butchering a pig so early?" Chen Ying would say, or, cursing the crows on a tree, "Quiet down! You inauspicious birds!" Shanzi grew reluctant to practice.

One day, Shanzi followed the women villagers loosening soil on the hills for seeding corn and wheat. Around mid-morning, the women took an extended break as they often did. Shanzi had just finished digging her row of dirt when Chen Ying walked past her. Chen Ying always carried her baby on her back at work, and lately had developed the habit of sitting on a hillside, away from the group, and breast-feeding. The baby girl, who had large curious eyes and red cheeks, rarely cried. As Chen Ying passed she took a sidelong look at Shanzi's work and smirked, but said nothing. Alerted, Shanzi called Zhou Sixth to check what she had done wrong. Zhou Sixth fiddled the soil with a hoe and showed Shanzi the hard ground under a shallow layer of loosened soil.

"That's called digging? Or cat covering shit?" A woman's words excited laughter among several others idling nearby. Shanzi's face went crimson. "I know I'm not good at this!" She threw the hoe on the ground and sat down on its grip.

Their lolling about was broken by Head Chen, who walked up with another man, and as the women rushed back to work, the two men approached Shanzi.

"Commune school's Sensei Guo," Head Chen said, introducing them.

The young man held out his hand. "I'm Guo Yujia, Shanzi. How have you been doing?" He smiled and, as they had that first day, his long eyes curved into crescents.

Shanzi hid dirty hands behind her back. "*Sensei*? That sounds like an old *pedant*." How did such a glib tongue come so naturally? She had met this man only once, and briefly, but she spoke to him like he was one of her own.

Guo Yujia beamed. "I am a *pedant* indeed, just not old." His laughter made the other women rubberneck, whispering with heads down. Head Chen told Shanzi that her job today was to help survey paddy fields. "Cooperate with Sensei Guo," he ordered and left.

Trouser legs rolled up to his thighs, Guo Yujia, joined by the village accountant, trudged in water and mud, measuring each edge of a field with pre-scaled bamboo poles. All Shanzi had to do was stay dry on the ridge, drawing the shape of each field, jotting each edge's length as Guo Yujia sang it out. She even calculated the area of each polygon without being asked, and still had time to move to the next field. She realized, with trepidation, that she enjoyed this — more than the drudgery of the fields. Oh! Did she just think the word *drudgery*? Such a bourgeois thought! Quickly she concentrated on the job.

For lunch, she invited Yujia to her room, though Yujia had brought two cold steamed buns with him. She couldn't find fresh vegetables to cook, so Yujia shared his buns and she shared her boiled water. He noticed her bookshelf and asked permission to look. He drew out several books, and wanted to borrow *300 Poems of the Tang Dynasty*, one of her favorites. The book was wrapped in brown Kraft paper.

"How did you pick that one?" She asked, surprised.

"Covered books are usually the interesting ones." Then he saw the flute with its gold-and-red tassel, hanging on the wall. He asked her to play and she did. First a popular flute solo, the fast-paced, prideful piece, "I Am a Soldier."

He shook his head. "Not my cup of tea. A pedant can't reason with a soldier, you know."

She chuckled and blew another, the lyrical "Shepherd Girl."

He nodded. "Better. Any more that are better still?"

"What's your idea of better?"

"Like a Tang Dynasty poem."

She tilted her head. After a moment she said, "I know. You must like 'Spring River, Blossoms, and Moon Night.' But I haven't practiced. How about next time?"

He agreed.

Walking out one after the other, they bumped into a crowd of village kids eavesdropping at the door. The kids dispersed in all directions like frightened sparrows. Shanzi and Yujia looked at each other and smiled.

The afternoon went fast. The off-gong hammered and people ran to their family plots. By the time the sun set, only one more field remained to be measured and Shanzi wished the village had more. Just then, she heard screaming.

"My baby! Oh heavens, my baby fell off the cliff!"

Shanzi saw Chen Ying alone on the hill, flailing both arms. Yujia and the accountant turned around in the mud, alarmed. She dropped her notebook and ran toward the screams.

On the hill, Chen Ying covered her mouth and pointed to the cliff, as if afraid to look down. Shanzi kneeled at the edge and saw a hill full of bamboo plants, old and young, thick and thin, like thousands of soldiers and horses charging down a battlefield. A baby carrier rolled with uneven speed between bamboo trunks and wild grass, silently disappearing as she watched.

But the hill was not too steep. Here and there Shanzi saw sizable spots on which to land her feet, the first one about two meters down. She asked herself if she dared to jump — like the ten-year-old she was when she practiced flying with arms open. *Yes.* She jumped.

For a while she was unable to anchor her feet and kept sliding downhill, until a large bamboo trunk stopped her and she could hold onto it and stand up. Feeling a rough burn on her face and hands, she looked down: the cliff suddenly opened, steep and bare, few plants along its walls. In shock, she sucked in cold air: Deep down, the baby carrier glinted among the rocks. She closed her eyes. The baby was finished.

"Shanzi!" Yujia called from above.

"I'm here. I'm fine." She started to climb back, alternating hands to grab bamboo plants. And then she saw a colorfully patched cotton blanket caught in a grove of young bamboo. The baby was lying on it! Awake and quiet, it rolled its black-bean eyes around, looking at the bamboo, the hill, the sky, then at Shanzi. The baby kicked its legs and waved its arms, and a smile crept across the little pink face. Shanzi held her own breath, carefully approached and wrapped the baby in the blanket.

At the top of the hill, Shanzi handed the baby to Chen Ying, wiped cold sweat off her forehead, and waited for thanks. Chen Ying threw her a venomous stare and hurried away, holding the baby tightly.

Shanzi touched her scraped face with a scratched hand and stood there, distracted. What had she done wrong? Had Chen Ying done this to get rid of the baby? Beside her, Guo Yujia stood by an aged peach tree, his legs muddy, his expression complicated. A gust of wind shook the tree branches, and the last petals fell and drifted down the hill.

Summer

The July sun had a magical power that made everything radiate a scent: the milky grains of rice, the corn stalks pregnant with their heavy ears, the crawling sweet potato vines. When Shanzi walked along the winding trail to the commune or returned to Lily Village, all kinds of mystic fragrances followed her, discernible at one moment and disappearing the next. The most distinct scent came from lotus leaves. If sunrays had a scent, Shanzi thought, it would be of lotus leaves.

What she liked about Zhou Sixth's family plot, small and unique in Lily Village, was that one third of it was watery mud. Above the mud stood hundreds of round lotus leaves — large plates, small umbrellas, or upside-down pot lids. Wind rolled water drops back and forth on the leaves, like crystal pearls. Here and there an enormous white or pink flower craned out on a long, thin stem, graceful and fresh like a young girl. Emerging from mud, smelling of sun.

"Why do you have more white flowers than pink?" Shanzi asked Zhou Sixth.

"Pink has nice seedpods. White gets good roots."

"Pink is prettier."

"Lotus roots sell well."

"Who do you sell them to?"

"The commune's dining room and the town people. Those public rice eaters really like lotus root dishes."

"Yeah, I like them too. Don't you?"

"Too much of a luxury for us peasants."

Soon Shanzi began scooping a bowl of raw rice and running to the Zhou family's kitchen, where she poured the rice into the boiling pot and requested "Lotus leaf gruel please."

Zhou Sixth's mother, a smiling old lady with white cloth wrapped around her head year-round, would scold, "Lazy worm!" and pick a fresh lotus leaf from under a pink flower, put two bamboo sticks across the pot on the top, and cover the pot with the round leaf. Steam would rise through the leaf, filling the kitchen with its delicate aroma. Sometimes the mother would also bring in a green, fresh seedpod, shaped like a shower nozzle and filled with white, peanut-like seeds, for Shanzi to munch.

One evening, Shanzi ran into Chen Ying on the way to Zhou's house. Chen Ying stared at Shanzi's rice bowl. "Zhou Sixth, the smarty, made such a good friend. Can you spare extra rice for me too?"

"This is for my own supper. . . ."

Chen Ying looked dubious and stalked off, the curious baby on her back.

At the supper table, Shanzi indulged in eating the fragrant lotus-leaf gruel with the Zhou family's pickled radishes. She ate with such relish it made Zhou Sixth's mother smile. Shanzi said, "Can you believe, I cooked one *jin*[1] solid rice and ate it in a single meal yesterday! That's three meals' quota!"

"Poor child," Zhou Sixth's mother sympathized. "Look what all this hard labor has done to you. How could your mother have the heart to let you go so far away alone?"

"She doesn't. She cried when she saw me off at the port. *I* didn't."

"Take it easy," Zhou Sixth said, "or your rice ration won't be enough."

Shanzi asked. "Auntie Zhou, do you always have watery gruel?"

"Eat watery in the slack season, eat solid in the busy season."

"Isn't this a busy season? I'm exhausted every day."

"Ah, you haven't seen the busiest time. Wait till next month when we reap the rice."

Zhou Sixth's younger brother left the table first, after pouring two bowls of thin gruel into his stomach, and was now in the corner chopping hogweeds for the pigs. He chipped in: "If I had your luck to get reborn in the city, I'd eat three solid meals a day, 360 days a year."

His sister reminded him that their elder brother's food ration made them better off. Be thankful. They could be like poor Jinling, whose wife Chen Ying took away all his rice.

"Why? Where did she take it?" Asked Shanzi.

"To her mother. Her mother's village is even poorer than ours."

Shanzi told them about her conversation with Chen Ying and asked, "Should I give her some rice?"

No one answered. Then the mother sighed. "One liter of rice makes a friend, ten liters of rice make an enemy."

---

1   1 *jin* = 0.5 kilograms

Every fifth day was market day, and Shanzi sometimes went with Zhou Sixth to sell lotus roots. Taking a break from hawking her wares, Zhou Sixth saw Shanzi sitting street-side, listening to children reading aloud in the commune school.

"Thinking of someone?"

"Nonsense," said Shanzi. But when the off-school bell rang at noon, she suddenly became attentive to the crowds passing by from the school's direction. Zhou Sixth, who just sold out her lotus roots, counted a small pile of dirty and wrinkled bills, licking her index finger from time to time.

"Not a bad day. Let's go home." Zhou Sixth threaded her pole through the empty baskets and placed it on her shoulder, biting a crunchy raw lotus root, "You want one?"

"Wait a moment . . ." Shanzi searched for an excuse to linger. "Why don't we go there for lunch?" She pointed to the Noodle House across the street.

Zhou Sixth held her moneybag tightly, shaking her head like a rattle: "No. No. Meat noodles cost 20 *fen* a bowl, more than a whole pound of salt."

Shanzi offered, "My treat. I just got money from my mother," not mentioning how little.

Zhou Sixth looked longingly at the Noodle House, whose cooking perfumed the air. Then she elbowed Shanzi. "Look who's there." Guo Yujia was walking through the crowd, a book under his arm, looking from one side of the street to the other.

Shanzi, catching up to him, asked, "Pedant, what are you looking for?"

Startled, he turned. "Oh, for . . . lotus roots." He pointed to Zhou Sixth's baskets.

Zhou Sixth said, "You always look but never buy."

"Oh? But I need to make sure our kitchen can find them. Shanzi, how are you doing?"

"Do I look like a laborer now?" Shanzi showed him the calluses on her palms.

"Don't try to get fat with one mouthful."

"I . . . wait, Zhou Sixth!" Shanzi noticed her friend slipping away. Zhou Sixth didn't stop.

"I have to go home to weed vegetables." Shanzi's eyes met Yujia's for a short moment, then cast down. "I must go with her." Her voice was soft, leaking sadness.

Long after the girls were gone, Yujia stood watching the path they had taken.

In August, the rice plants turned a billowing gold. After supper, when women cooked hogweeds and fed the pigs, men stood at the edge of their courtyard smoking tobacco leaves and chatting.

"Eaten?"

"Yeah. You?"

"Yeah."

"Looks like we got a good year."

"Well, a good year is never ours."

Harvest season came and went like a storm, leaving no time to think. The whole village went to battle, working like one person, all traces of laziness left behind. In field after field, silver sickles slashed up and down the golden paddies. One day plants were reaped, tied in bundles, and stood in the fields like scarecrows. Another day bundles were spread on the threshing grounds. All night, water buffalo pulled heavy granite rollers round the four threshing grounds. While the buffalo took breaks and men snorted in their beds, women beat the plants with flails, scratched away the straw with bamboo rakes, and winnowed the grain with shovels, taking only quick naps on piles of hot straw or pads of cool concrete. At last the golden grains of rice were separated from the straw, dried by the sun, and piled into the storage rooms.

One morning, Head Chen led the villagers to hand in public grain to the commune, Shanzi volunteered to join the force of mostly men. Zhou Sixth wouldn't go. "Got my period," she had whispered.

Everyone carried a pair of baskets of rice on a shoulder-pole, men carrying a hundred *jin* or more. At first Shanzi tried to carry a hundred *jin* too, but she couldn't stand up — it was more than her body weight. "Don't show off," Head Chen said with a frown, "I don't want the responsibility of you straining your back."

Shanzi scooped out some rice and poured it back to the storage pile. After testing a few times, she settled on seventy *jin*, about the same weight as the water buckets she carried every day. As the parade got ready to move, Shanzi went back to retrieve her straw hat. The yard was filled with men waiting, some sitting on the shoulder-poles laid across their loads of rice. She wove a path between the men, leaping over a shoulder-pole that no one sat on.

"Fuck your mother!" A curse sounded above her head like a low thunder. She spun around and saw Jinling's reddened face. The tallest man in the village and (according to rumors) one whose stomach never got properly filled, Jinling was usually pallid, lackadaisical, and almost never talked to Shanzi. She was so shocked by the sudden explosion of energy in his anger that she stood immobilized.

Chen Ying rushed over, the baby on her back. As soon as his wife neared, Jinling withdrew again, squatting in a corner, droopy as a frostbitten plant. Chen Ying untied Jinling's shoulder-pole from the baskets and pushed it into Shanzi's arms: "What in the hell are you doing? Flaunting your cunt?" Above the men's laughter, she continued to yell: "You are giving my man a shoulder ulcer! Wash this off!"

Shanzi's cheeks grew hot. She let the shoulder-pole fall on the ground. "That's superstition! And quit using dirty words, like a thug!"

Chen Ying spat hard and turned to the men watching this entertainment: "Old men, young men! Look at the city devil! She dared to call *me* names!" She pressed against Shanzi. "Dirty? You don't know what dirty thing I can do if you don't wash it. You wash it or not?"

Backing up a few steps from Chen Ying, shaking with anger, Shanzi realized at that moment that she was sorry she had ever come to this village.

Head Chen broke up the onlookers and ordered Chen Ying to shut up. He switched his own shoulder-pole with Jinling's and told Shanzi never to walk over a man's shoulder-pole again.

This incident lowered Shanzi's spirit. Unlike her relaxed walk to the commune on market days, the three-kilometer trail with a heavy load on her shoulder proved almost unbearable. Soaked in sweat, she had to switch shoulders many times and take many breaks before reaching the commune's grain station; by then, the other villagers had already come and gone.

To her surprise, Secretary Xia was there himself, weighing each basket of grain on a platform scale. He praised Shanzi, "You are the best insert!" That lifted her spirit. She looked around for other inserts, but saw none in the crowd. Secretary Xia asked casually, "Is it a good year in Lily Village?"

"I think so," Shanzi answered, thinking of the four storage rooms full of shining golden grain.

"Do you know how much rice your village produced?"

"Hmm, not sure. Our accountant must have the record. Didn't Head

Chen already tell you?"

"Oh, I just want to double check. In recent years your village's production had been quite low. You know, if this year's production exceeded the National Agriculture Standard, that's not only your village's glory, it is also our commune's glory."

Shanzi got interested: "How high is the Standard?"

"For our area, it's five hundred *jin* of rice per *mu*.[2] "

"I can measure the storage rooms and compute it," Shanzi offered, glad to have a chance to use her math skills, perhaps even Mr. Tan's calculus book. "Can I tell you next market day?"

"Sure. You can always find me in the commune's office. By the way, do you have enough rice to eat?"

Shanzi first nodded, then shook her head a little.

Secretary Xia reached his pocket and took out a small bill, "Take this. Even the smartest housewife can't cook a meal without rice." Quoting the folk adage, he laughed heartily. The bill was a 5-*jin* rice ticket, with which one could buy rice from the commune's grain station. It was still new. Shanzi hesitated.

"That's your ration. Don't you need it too?" She said.

"I have a small stomach. Take it. You kids are eating growth food."

Shanzi felt grateful to Secretary Xia; he was a nice leader. His generosity lessened the pain in her blistered shoulders.

The next market day, hardly able to contain her excitement, Shanzi arrived at Secretary Xia's office. "I computed it! Our rice production really exceeded the Agriculture Standard! It's about 520 *jin* per *mu*! Are you going to award our village?"

Secretary Xia's eyes immediately shone. In a swish he stood up, as if going to do something right away, then sat down again behind his desk.

"Sure. Good job, Shanzi." His voice was too flat. Shanzi felt disappointed.

"Did you tell anyone that you were coming to see me?" Secretary Xia asked.

"No."

He suggested they not tell the village, but surprise them. Then he asked if she would be a night-school instructor.

"Are we going to start a night-school?"

"Yes. This is the Party and Chairman Mao's instruction. We are launching

2　　1 *mu* = 0.164 acre

a campaign to eliminate illiteracy."

At that moment Shanzi realized that for the half year since she had come to the countryside, she hadn't thought much about the world revolution. She had been too busy dealing with the chores of everyday life — just like her mother, whom she had never wanted as a role model.

Secretary Xia said, "We will first start by making Lily Village a pilot night school. The time you spend teaching will count toward work points. Why don't you report to Guo Yujia first? He is the general instructor."

"Oh?"

"He recommended you as an instructor."

"Thanks," her voice stayed calm but her heart beat faster.

Fall

The fifteenth day of the eighth month in the lunar calendar is the Moon Festival. On that day in September the Commune of New Wonders called for the first meeting of all night-school instructors, held in the commune's conference hall. Afterward, Guo Yujia asked Shanzi to stay a little longer to discuss the night-school business. Instead, he handed her the *300 Poems of the Tang Dynasty*.

"That's it?" Shanzi said.

"So beautiful," Yujia said.

"What is beautiful?"

"The poems."

"Oh. Yes."

"Do you want to stay for supper in the commune's dining room?"

"Don't you worry about gossip?"

"What's there to gossip about? The general instructor treating his subordinate?"

"Okay, then."

They had supper in the commune's dining room, together with other cadres and schoolteachers — all "public rice eaters," as Zhou Sixth called them. The kitchen indeed offered a dish with lotus roots, and Shanzi happily ordered it. Yujia paid for their meals with his meal tickets.

As they walked out of the dining room, the sun was setting, and the outline of the full moon was already visible in the sky. Yujia walked Shanzi to the end of the town's street. They stood under the huge umbrella of a flowering sweet-olive tree, its blossoms swarms of tiny, rice-size yellow pistils hidden in saw-toothed dark green leaves, its perfume pure and placid, somewhat mysterious, even unpredictable, like autumn itself.

Yujia said, "Bye, Shanzi. See you again."

"When?"

"Soon, I hope."

Shanzi hid her disappointment and said goodbye. Walking down the winding trail, she left the floating fragrance of sweet-olive behind. Halfway to Lily Village she saw that the full moon, hanging like a silver plate over the darkened hills and fields, had risen to the middle of the sky, turning the stone road white. Shanzi glanced at her book and saw the red tassel of a bookmark. She hadn't put a bookmark in it. She stopped, opened to that page and read the poem under the moonlight:

Watching the Moon on the Night of Fifteenth
by Wang Jian

Ground is white, crows dwelling on tree
Cold dews wet sweet-olive with nothing to say
Tonight all look up at the bright moon
Autumn longing fall on whose home?

Shanzi read it a number of times and ruminated. It was a poem she had been able to recite since elementary school. She resumed her walk, but stopped once again. In the quiet of the nightly wilderness, she yelled to the full moon, "*Yes!*"

Turning around she ran, her cotton shoes drumming up the stony road. Fifteen minutes later she was back at the edge of the town. She slowed down and walked to the sweet-olive tree. Sure enough, Guo Yujia stood under it, hands behind his back like an elementary student facing the teacher.

"Pedant, why are you so nasty?" Shanzi said, still breathing hard, "making me run back from a wasted trip?"

In the shadows of the tree, she couldn't see Yujia's face clearly, but could feel his smiling eyes. He said, "I wasn't sure if I was too imprudent."

"What have you been doing while I was gone?"

"Climbing the tree, picking flowers for you." He revealed his hands from behind his back, and presented her a bouquet of sweet-olive blossoms.

Instead of taking the flowers, Shanzi took the hand that held the bouquet and ran. Yujia kept pace with her. In one breath they reached the outskirts of the town, a massive area of harvested rice fields.

"No one comes to the empty fields in the night. We are safe." Shanzi let go of Yujia's hand, took the bouquet, and sat down on the ridge between two fields. Yujia followed, sitting down beside her.

They sat shoulder to shoulder and looked up at the moon, just as the poem said. From time to time Shanzi held the sweet-olive bouquet to her nose as if she could not have enough of its fragrance.

"What are you thinking now, Shanzi?" Yujia asked, ever so gently.

"Wondering what my mom is doing."

"What does your family do on Moon Festival evening?"

"Eat moon cakes in the yard . . . I wish I had one now."

From his baggy pocket, Yujia took something wrapped with white waxed paper. He placed it in Shanzi's palm.

"How did you get that?" she cried with joy. She unwrapped a corner of the paper, smelled the Suzhou moon cake, carefully wrapped it again, and put it in her pocket.

"Don't you want to eat it now?"

"I want to share it with Zhou Sixth tomorrow. Is that okay?"

"Oh yes, please." He paused, then asked, "Have you ever fallen in love with someone before?"

"No . . . but . . ." Shanzi thought of Mr. Tan, and flushed.

"Yes! Who was it?"

"I don't think it was love. He was at least thirty years older. I just don't know why, sometimes, I felt sentimentally attached to him."

"He was your teacher," Yujia said.

"How do you know?"

"I am a teacher too, remember? Did you feel you wanted to be with him all the time, like I feel toward you?"

"Not really . . . actually there was strange pleasure in saying good-bye. It's kind of like reading a distressing little poem, you want to luxuriate in the distress. . . ."

Yujia laughed quietly. "You are right, that wasn't love, just a crush. It's pretty common for girls in their mid-teens."

"How do you know?"

"I read psychology books. Most interesting. I can get you one if you want."

"Aren't those books *four olds* and forbidden?" she said, referring to *old thought, old culture, old tradition,* and *old custom.* "Where did you get them?"

"This is *four olds* also," Yujia pointed to the Tang poem book in Shanzi's hand. "You tell me first. Where did you get it?"

"I was ten when the Cultural Revolution started, and my father asked me to help him burn all his books. I hid this one," Shanzi looked at the moon. "He still doesn't know."

Shanzi rested her head on Yujia's shoulder, a natural pillow. Yujia tilted his face toward hers, gently rubbing her cheek with his own. His body slowly turned and his lips approached hers, but Shanzi dodged away and buried her face in her hands.

"Do you not want to?" Yujia took her hand.

"What will others say?"

"I don't care."

"Not now. Yujia, let's just sit here and talk, okay?"

"So when?"

"When there is no moon, so it can't see us."

"Oh you are so . . . pure." Yujia sighed. "You really don't want it tonight?"

Shanzi pulled back her hand and did not answer.

"Are you mad?" Yujia sounded frightened, "I'm sorry, I didn't mean . . ."

"No," Shanzi whispered, "it's just that . . . I don't want our first . . . kiss . . . so easily. . . ."

"I understand," Yujia whispered back. "Whenever you are ready."

"Perhaps on my birthday. . . ."

"Which day is that?"

"October first, National Day."

"I can wait two weeks. Just two weeks, no more, okay?"

"Okay."

They sat quietly, shoulder to shoulder again, until the night dew moistened their clothes, and then they walked slowly along the ridge between the paddies. Neither wanted to say good night.

"Do you want to meet a friend of mine?" Yujia asked.

She nodded.

"Come with me. But promise you'll never tell anybody!"

"I promise!" Shanzi said. She loved secrets, and this was Yujia's secret!

They left the fields, walked in moonlight along the bus road paved with crushed stones. Ten minutes later, Yujia brought her onto a side path that led to a large village. He pointed to a red-walled house, big as a mansion. "That's Secretary Xia's home."

"How come he has such a nice house when peasants don't even have enough to eat?"

"That's the value of his position," Yujia said quietly. "Why do you think he presses the peasants so hard for everything?"

They headed deeper into the large village and entered a courtyard, setting all the dogs to barking. Yujia knocked on a door, and Shanzi saw a shadow moving across a paper-covered window. A man holding an oil lamp opened the door.

"Good evening, Sensei," Yujia said.

Shanzi covered her mouth and chuckled. She still was not used to hearing this old-fashioned title.

"Aha, uninvited guests. How are you doing, Yujia? 'Several days unseen, as if three autumns.' I see you have company."

"Yes, Sensei, I hope you don't mind that I brought over a trusted friend without asking you first."

"Yujia, your friend is my friend, you know that."

Shanzi followed Yujia into the house: messy as a pigpen, it lacked a woman's touch. The full-bearded host grabbed dirty laundry from chairs and invited them to sit. He looked like a caveman.

Yujia said, "Shanzi came to see your books, if you don't mind."

"Oh, please. Of course." The man pulled open a wall-size curtain of white homespun cloth and held up the oil lamp over Shanzi's head, lighting rows of books on unpainted wooden shelves. In contrast with the messy house, the books were arranged so neatly that, for a moment, the green and gold volumes reminded Shanzi of a magnificent library. She studied the shelves hungrily.

"Ah, so many. How did you collect all these forbidden books?"

"My insert friends. Whenever they go to the city, they bring a book or two for me. Those who leave the countryside leave me their collections."

"How can you hide so many books under Secretary Xia's eyelids?"

"Haven't you heard that the safest place to hide is in your enemy's castle? One must take risks."

Shanzi felt uneasy, hearing the word "enemy" associated with Secretary Xia, but she thought about the red-walled mansion and then, too, Zhou Sixth's words about taking sides. She needed more time to think.

"How can you find the time to read all these books?" she said, feeling strange that she hadn't touched a book for quite a while. Not even the calculus book from Teacher Tan. She had been living like a primitive farmer, going to labor at sunrise and going to bed at sunset.

"Reading is all I do," the man replied.

"You don't do labor at all?" Shanzi asked in disbelief.

"That's right. I just stay here and read all day, sometimes all night."

"What about your work points?"

"Aha, work points. How much are a day's work points worth in your village?"

"Eight *fen* . . ." Shanzi murmured. A day's work was not even enough to buy a steamed bun, which cost ten *fen*. Not willing to retreat, she quizzed him. "How do you eat? If you don't have work points, you don't get any grain after harvest."

"My parents and sisters send money and rice tickets they save for me from the city."

"You don't feel ashamed, depending on your family? Such a big man, unable to earn your own rice?"

"Shanzi!" Yujia touched her hand.

"No worries, Yujia." The man said calmly, "Let her speak her mind." He turned to Shanzi again. "Do you know any villager's family that has more food than your family in the city?"

That stopped Shanzi's tongue. To be honest, the answer was no.

"We are taking raw food from the peasants' mouths, young lady! They don't have much left after handing in public grain, and still we take away more."

Shanzi stared at the host. What was he saying? Head Chen's stern face, his little girl's hungry eyes, Jinling's tired figure, Chen Ying's grudging glance . . . all a result of what she was part of? Next year and who knew how many years hence, she would be robbing food from Chen Ying, Zhou Sixth . . . from all of them?

"We are the intruders," the host continued without mercy. "Do you know why we had to come to the countryside?"

Teacher Tan had asked her the same question, such a simple question, and she thought she knew the answer. Now it didn't seem so simple. "Why?"

"Because there are no jobs in the city for us. We are all unemployed. Millions and millions of us, and the burden is transferred to the peasants."

"*Unemployed*," Shanzi repeated in shock. Throughout her education, that term had applied only to capitalist countries, like imperialist America.

She had never connected this concept with the great movement of "up the mountains and down to the countryside." A huge unemployed population in China, the greatest socialist country on earth? The steel wall of support for the third world?

"Do you mean . . . *they* have made our country worse?" she asked with apparent hesitation.

"*They*, and *us*."

"Us?"

"You and me. With our young, hot blood; our innocent, loyal belief. With our lofty spirit, our revolution tried to go north by driving the chariot southward." He did not raise his voice on any of the sentimental adjectives that Shanzi's generation had grown up hearing, nor did he sound ironic. This made his words hit harder.

Shanzi slowly sat down by the table, where the little flame of another oil lamp glittered. She held her cheeks with both hands. The man patted a book; on its hard cover were printed a few bold characters: *The Social Contract,* by Rousseau.

As they walked out of the caveman's house, Shanzi was unusually quiet.

"Who is he?" she asked after awhile.

"Once a leader of the Red Guard in your city," Yujia said, and told her the name. She recognized it right away. It had been on everyone's lips a few years ago, a synonym for heroism.

She fell silent again, then said, "I feel uneasy about one thing."

Yujia held her hand. "Tell me."

" I told Secretary Xia about our rice production. I thought the accountant might have computed it wrong. But . . . it just occurred to me, things are not that simple."

Yujia jerked his foot back from its next step. "You what?"

Shanzi looked at him in the moonlight and said defensively, "I didn't mean to hurt them."

Yujia resumed walking, still holding her hand. He said nothing and Shanzi began to feel frightened. She asked, "How bad is it?"

"The villagers will really hate you if they find out. I think you should go back to the city for a while."

"What? No! I'm not going to be a deserter! The night school is about to start! Besides, I can't hide in the city forever. I will find a chance to explain it to them."

Yujia sighed. He patted Shanzi's hand. "Don't say a thing before we figure out how to say it, okay?"

The next market day, Shanzi met Yujia in the commune and discussed what to say to the villagers. She felt a little better when she returned to the village in the afternoon. Hard as it would be, she would confess to Head Chen and Zhou Sixth. She would accept their blame and figure out a remedy for the damage, even if it meant lying to Secretary Xia. It simply made no sense to her that a man living in a red-walled mansion had the right to take grain from people who didn't have enough to eat.

Only she was one step late. That morning, while she was still in the commune, Secretary Xia sent a representative to appear at Lily Village's cadre meeting. When the representative arrived, Head Chen and the village accountant were discussing grain distribution, having turned in all the public grain. Half a storage room of rice remained, and that abundance had made the villagers laugh and talk louder.

The commune cadre, however, delivered Secretary Xia's instruction for Lily Village to hand in more public grain and fulfill the government designated proportion of their actual production. He told them it was a crime to conceal a portion of the crop, but as long as they handed in the full amount of their allotment, the commune would not take further action against them. He left the village cadres in misery.

The news spread instantly through the four courtyards of Lily Village. In the next few hours, Jinling ran away to the leper village, and his wife, Chen Ying, wailed in despair, telling all assembled that her husband had been lying in bed without any food for two days, there being not a grain of rice in their house. They had been waiting for the grain distribution. Following the village cadre meeting, Jinling got up and left, saying that at least the lepers didn't have to pay public grain.

Shanzi walked into her courtyard as a rioting crowd piled at Chen Ying's door. She could only see people's heads and backs, and couldn't make out words in the flurry of the upset voices. Instinctively, she sensed this had to do with her mistake. She stood behind the crowd, heart palpitating, and tried to make sense of the hubbub. Then she caught the word *insert* and Chen Ying's shrill, "Where's the city devil? Where is she?"

As if on a command, the crowd moved swiftly to either side, forming a lane. Chen Ying appeared at her door, hair disheveled, hands in fists, eyes reddened.

Where is her baby, Shanzi thought. The next instant she confronted Chen Ying's eyes, burning with naked hatred — for Shanzi, for poverty, and for hopelessness — such hatred as Shanzi had only seen directed at class enemies in revolutionary movies. For the first time Shanzi read Chen Ying's expression perfectly. She saw a reality that would never be taught in school. Sorrow overtook her, and she whispered to no one, "I'm sorry. . . ."

Chen Ying yelled, "You bitch! I'll tear you to pieces!" She charged across the high threshold and leapt, all teeth and claws. The crowd poured after her. Before Shanzi could respond, Zhou Sixth darted out and elbowed Shanzi so hard that she staggered. "Get out of here!" Zhou Sixth hissed; her words could barely be heard. Shanzi ran as fast as she could to her own room, almost stumbling over the doorsill. Once inside, she crossed the door's bars, blocked the chicken hole, and bolted the wood-board window. She stood in the middle of her bedroom breathing rapidly.

Outside, Chen Ying's cries rose over villagers' curses. A young man bashed at Shanzi's door, shouting, "Insert! You have the guts to be a traitor, but no guts to face us? Come out! Let us teach you a lesson!"

Inside, Shanzi mumbled, "I'm not a traitor."

The crowd yelled, "Let her be the last of her line!" "Hammer her flat!" "Drive her away!"

Zhou Sixth's anxious scream was first loud and nearby, "Head! Head! Where are you hiding?" Then her voice faded. Someone in the courtyard said that Head had gone to stop Jinling. Shanzi hoped her friend would get Head Chen back in time to stop the insane crowd.

She tried to block out the noise, thinking instead of Yujia, as if the dear thoughts of him could get her out of this predicament. She clung to thinking of another secret date, a week away. *I should have let him kiss me. . . .*

The yard seemed to be quieter. Had they finally tired of shouting and left? Shanzi stood on tiptoe and peeked from a crack in a window board. The peasants had not left. Instead they had weapons: hoes, sickles, ropes, and shoulder-poles. More people had come from the village. What were they going to do? She remembered a story that Zhou Sixth's mother had told, about a young man and a girl many years ago. The two young people had the same family name, and they violated the village's rule when they secretly fell in love. They were caught one autumn night making love in a pile of straw.

The villagers tied up the two naked youngsters and ordered them to kneel down in front of a large bonfire. The older peasants then took turns all night, scolding and beating them, giving an example to all the young people in the village. The next day, the girl jumped off a cliff. The young man ran away and had never been heard from again.

Shanzi had mourned for the young couple, but thought it an ancient story. Now she didn't know that these people from the same village wouldn't do the same thing to her. After all, she had violated their unwritten rule that no one tell the commune the village's true production.

She heard a new commotion in the yard. Panicked, needing to escape, she unbarred the back door. It faced a hill, and she could take the secluded path along the cliffs, then make a detour to the trail that led to the commune. She would be safe as soon as she found Yujia. Together they would figure out what to do.

She slipped out the back door. Within minutes, the villagers saw her and cried out. They chased her, like cats chasing a mouse along the cliff. Once upon a time when she was a little girl, Shanzi had often played cat-and-mice with the neighborhood children, and it was more fun to be a mouse. Today the mouse offered no match for the cats. She could hear heavy breathing as they closed in on her.

With no escape, Shanzi's fear turned to determination. She stopped abruptly and spun around. "Uncles and aunts," she called out to the approaching villagers. "Please let me explain. It was a mistake! I can help you! I have an idea. Let's discuss . . ." Before she finished, a shoulder-pole slammed into her leg and spit landed on her face. She groaned, falling on the ground, spit running into her eyes.

"Lose your fucking sweet lies!" "Who wants to discuss with a spy?" A roar of enraged curses and spit and fists fell on her from three sides. She curled up, using her arms to shield her head.

Eventually, the blows ceased. A murmur ran through the crowd and those in back dispersed. Shanzi lowered her arms and saw a blood-colored sunset — so brilliant and dazzling — before a final kick rolled her off the edge of the cliff.

A week later in the city, on National Day, scurrying through the deceptively cheerful sounds of gongs, drums and firecrackers, Mr. Tan arrived at the hospital.

Shanzi's mother sat alone, weeping beside her resting daughter. Seeing Mr. Tan, she wiped her eyes and pulled over a chair. He greeted her and went closer to look at Shanzi. Her eyes were wide open, but she didn't seem to see him. Mr. Tan called softly, "Classmate Shanzi." Her eyeballs did not move.

"She has not talked at all since she woke up in the commune's infirmary," Shanzi's mother said.

Mr. Tan asked to talk to the mother alone. In the hall, he asked what the doctor had said. There was a brain damage, said the mother.

"Will she recover?" Mr. Tan asked anxiously.

"The doctor is not sure. She was well when I saw her off eight months ago. . . . It's her birthday today. . . . " Shanzi's mother teared up again.

Mr. Tan wiped his glasses. A couple of years back, he had asked Shanzi a question in math class. Shanzi stood up and said mischievously, "I don't know the answer." "I know you do. Others pretend they know when they don't. You pretend you don't when you do," he had scolded her.

He wished she were only pretending now. If she would only wake up, he would never scold her again. He put his glasses back on, and walked inside with Shanzi's mother. They sat silently by either side of Shanzi's bed.

Shanzi's nostrils twitched, as if smelling something. Mr. Tan looked around, but did not see flowers in the small room. He had come in haste as soon as he heard about Shanzi's incident from another student, and hadn't brought flowers himself.

Shanzi's face turned slightly toward the door. Mr. Tan walked out again and looked around the hallway. No one was there except a nurse pushing a cart clinking with drug bottles. He was about to close the door when he saw the bouquet on the floor, in front of the door. A fresh bouquet of sweet-olive. The city did not have sweet-olive trees.

He picked up the bouquet, inhaling the delicate scent. He thought not of sweet-olive, but of winter plum, and saw an exuberant young girl shutting his door with the flick of a foot and asking him to find a vase — a girl who could have been a great mathematician. Teacher Tan stood remembering, before taking the bouquet inside to Shanzi's nightstand.

* * *

The Cultural Revolution lasted two more years, ending one month after Chairman Mao's death. The next year, in the autumn of 1977, the front-page of China's official national newspaper, *The People's Daily*, proclaimed that the mathematician Chen Jingrun had proved the preliminary 1+2 portion of Goldbach's Conjecture. That is, he proved that any even number can be expressed as the sum of a prime and a product of no more than two primes. The reporting of this mathematical achievement, the first of its kind in a decade, created a national furor.

In that same year all inserts — most no longer teenagers — were allowed to return to the cities legally, and universities in China were reopened. Many of Shanzi's former high school classmates passed the entrance exams and walked through the university gates. She was not among them.

Several months after the Red Guard hero-turned-caveman returned to the city seeking a proper job, he was arrested and would remain in jail for 15 years without a trial. His crime, committed a decade earlier, was leading an "armed fight" against an opposing faction of the Red Guard, one of the many fights that had resulted in casualties on both sides as children-turned-warriors vowed to defend Chairman Mao with their fresh blood.

Far from the city, the ex-head of Lily village, Head Chen, was imprisoned in the county jail for sabotaging the great movement of "city youths go up to mountains and down to the country."

To this day, Goldbach's Conjecture, the problem of 1+1, remains unsolved. #

THE RANDOMNESS OF LOVE

Many years ago in the countryside's winter field, a boy — also an "insert" sent down from the city — hugged me, both of us in thick, fashionable paramilitary greatcoats. Other than the pressure against my clothes, I felt nothing. Still I worried. "Did we do anything wrong?" I asked him. He let me go and replied in an annoyed voice, "No, girl! We haven't done the wrong thing yet!"

A few days after that hug, I got a stomachache. It was not like any pain I'd ever felt. I was unable to work in the field, yet I did not dare go see a doctor in the commune. From morning to evening I lay on my bed alone; under the cover I stroked my smooth belly skin with increasing panic. I tried to determine if my stomach had grown bigger but I couldn't tell. The unnamed fear tortured me far worse than the pain itself. A few more days passed and the pain gradually went away. I breathed out in relief, still confused by what the boy meant by "the wrong thing." I was eighteen. My passion had been for other matters then; I had purposes in life, purposes that I have since lost.

Nearly a decade later, one summer evening a friend asked me to go with her to a ballroom. I had recently graduated from an engineering college, and my mother had knocked on all her backdoors to secure me a job in our city. She made sure I would not leave home again, as I had done at 17. My official assignment was as a technician in a local factory, a place that needed neither a college graduate nor a technician. And switching jobs was not allowed. As Chairman Mao had — before he passed — repeatedly put it, each of us is just a gear or screw on the revolution machine, and must stay fixed wherever the Party places us. My job and life were so boring that the idea of going to a dance actually seemed exciting.

The ballrooms were a new fashion in town. I had never been in one before and it was curious to stand near the windows, where all the young women waited for an invitation to dance. As the *Blue Danube* washed lyrically on, a young man approached us and asked my friend to dance. She timidly placed her left hand on his shoulder and her body turned slightly away, but the waltz ended before their first steps. The two stood waiting in the middle of the dance floor, his arm on her waist and her hand on his shoulder, like a statue. Just when the music restarted, this time the *Friendship as Long as Earth and Heaven*, my friend suddenly pulled her hand off her partner's shoulder as if burned, and she giggled, covering her face with both hands. As she kept giggling, I was baffled; the whole room was baffled, and for a while no one danced, all eyes were on her. This attention made her more bashful so she ran from her dance partner and back to me. Before she could regain herself and before I could comfort her, a second man approached and asked her to dance. She sheepishly went with him while I remained in my spot — no one came to invite me. A new song began and a man walked toward me; almost within reach, he glanced up at my face but continued to walk past me and led another girl to the dance floor. I stood by myself through two or three more songs, and started to feel strange. I turned around to look into the window glass. The girlish round face mirrored in the glass did not seem too ugly, even without make-up. The slender figure in the reflection looked fine. So what was it in me that scared off men? I might be a female nerd in conversation, but how could they know this when I had yet to say a word?

When I was in the countryside, my neighbor talked to me only once. In the village I was "inserted" into, a pigpen separated my room from my neighbor's. The pigs belonged to the village head. Over the years I had gradually grown used to the oinks and the smell, although I still feared falling into the big opening of the latrine when going into the pigpen to relieve myself. My neighbor and I were both urban high school graduates who were sent down by the government into this farm production team. He was from the local county, while I was from the big city up the Yangtze River. Most of the year my neighbor was not in the village. He showed up only during food-distribution in the fall after harvest. Even when he was there he did not go to labor in the fields. He would either lie lazily under the sun reading a book, playing his Erhu instrument, or having a Go match with a friend from another village. He talked to me only once. He asked me why I stayed in the village year-round without going back to my city. I replied sincerely that I wanted to root myself in this poor farmland. He tried to hide his laughter, which made me feel I needed to explain things to him.

"Do you know?" I said. "All other countries in the world have population flowing from the countryside to the cities; only China is practicing the opposite. Our population flows from the cities to the countryside. This is a creative revolutionary movement, and its historical significance can never be overestimated. We are making history and I am proud to be part of it."

His grin gradually shifted to astonishment, and he walked away as if I were running loose from a mental hospital. I watched his back with sympathy and sighed over his poor spirit, a spirit with no purpose in life.

The men in the ballroom didn't know this, of course.

My friend had been dancing non-stop and finally came back to take a break. She looked completely gratified, her face red-hot and misted with fine sweat. When she saw me standing there, alone, her eyes opened wide projecting ten thousand question marks. She asked me why I did not dance. I was agape, and tongue-tied, and could not respond. I waited until she once again merged into the crowd on another man's arm before I escaped. A ballroom was not my place and I would never go to one again. On the way out, I thought hard about how I once excelled in math, English and philosophy, to pillar my faltering self-esteem.

On the way home I walked past a door that I had been familiar with for years. It was still early so I decided to drop by and pay a long-due visit to a friend from my time in the countryside. Because he was the oldest among the "city inserts," we all called him "Old Brother." The rest of us were new to the countryside, young and far away from parents, so it was he who gave us advice and tips on how to cope. The remote memory of his kindness in the alien countryside warmed me. I wanted his help to figure out my current dilemma. More specifically, I wanted to ask if he knew why the boy I fell in love with in college stopped seeing me before our first kiss; instead he mailed me a letter that said "You are a woman too outstanding — perhaps this is exactly your own tragedy." This calm analysis made me long for mediocrity. I feared that something odd in my bones had somehow leaked out to my face, something that caused even strange men in the ballroom to sulk away at the sight of it without me saying a word.

Old Brother's door was ajar, and a hubbub of voices inside floated out through the crack. After two knocks with no answer, I pushed the door open. In the haze of light-blue smoke I saw several bare-shouldered men in their mid-thirties cracking sunflower seeds and chatting. Some faces looked familiar. A buzzing floor fan slowly stirred the hot air, a mix of cigarettes and sweat, a much better smell than the ballroom's competing perfumes. It aroused memories of a small messy room in the countryside, where I argued red-faced with male inserts on national and world politics. Well, at that time cigarettes were rare luxury stuff, so the boys mostly smoked dry tobacco leaves like the farmers. The tang from the cloud they blew was much stronger than this, but I never disliked it.

Old Brother greeted me as if he had just seen me yesterday, and made a man move to offer me a seat. "She's a university graduate," he told everyone. I sat down among the men, ignoring curious glances. The noise level of their chat dropped a notch or two and some put on their T-shirts. A few moments later I realized that they had been talking about their first loves in the countryside; their language grew more civil with me there, their disconsolation somewhat more strained. Why couldn't they continue to use their true voices? I felt again like an interloper.

A door banged behind me and I turned around to see a man walking out of the bathroom zipping his fly. As I averted my eyes, I heard Old Brother telling the man a lady was present.

"Is she Chair*woman* Mao?" The zipper asked without any hint of smile.

I tried to hold my cheeks tight but failed. Unladylike laughter burst out with a flow of released energy from my jammed chest. All the men laughed at my laughter, their heads swaying to and fro. This made me laugh harder. I finally wiped my tears when Old Brother handed me a cup of tea. He lowered his head, smiled at me with familiar caring eyes, and asked softly how I planned to spend this weekend. I told him I was going to hike the South Mountains.

"Alone?" he asked.

"Unless your wife lets you go with me," I said.

"How about I go with you?" A man stood between Old Brother and me. I looked up and saw the wise guy from the bathroom. Who had cut his hair? I nearly said this out loud. His rumpled hair, pale face, and the old handloom cloth shirt showed a man who cared less about appearance than I did. Lowering my eyes, I saw his ill-fitting pants, one leg shorter than the other. His humility somehow eased the strangeness between us.

He sat by me without invitation. "I am a fortuneteller," he said, "I see a word written between your eyebrows."

I was expecting another joke; instead I was startled at his observation. The word was *death*; I said it instantly. I knew this because Guan Lu, the legendary diviner and *I-Ching* interpreter in the Three Kingdom Period, once saw a father and son plowing a field, and told them the 19-year-old son would die within three days. Guan Lu's divine eyes had read the word "death" between the young man's eyebrows. Begged by the father to save his son's life, Guan Lu taught the young man to bribe the gods of North Dipper and South Dipper as they played a match of Go. The boy secretly provided them with wine and venison. After they had consumed the wine and meat the boy made himself known and asked for a favor. The gods added the character "nine" on top of "nineteen" by his name in the life-and-death book, so the young man's life span was changed from 19 to 99.

"No," he said, taken aback by my reaction. Then he slowly spelled "loneliness" and gazed at me. I exhaled with relief.

"You know *The Three Kingdoms* well?" he said. "That's not a book for ladies. A lady who reads books like that . . . be prepared for a rough and bumpy road ahead. It doesn't matter how much you have been spoiled by life so far."

I wanted to laugh, but stopped short. There was a strange seriousness in his gaze. As to his fortune-telling skill, he was wrong — I didn't have the luxury to be spoiled. Never before, not now. Most likely not ever. But I said nothing. My heart was softened by his words even though I felt this was exactly the wrong reaction. No one other than my mother had cared about my fate before. For some unknown reason everyone seemed to regard me as a girl too strong and too smart to need any help or care. This was how it had always been.

I turned my eyes away from him, in time to hear the others announce that they were going to stay up and talk right through the night. Old

Brother's wife was out of town and would not return until tomorrow — a golden opportunity for an overnight chat party. Old Brother mentioned I was welcome to stay too. I glanced at the "fortuneteller" and saw the expectation in his eyes. It was time to leave, I thought, but I didn't move.

So I stayed with them in a roomful of smoke, talked and teased and laughed as if drunk from the tea, sunflower seeds, and cigarettes. It was like the old times with my fellow inserts in the countryside. Old Brother served the tenth round of tea as his wall clock struck midnight. We continued to chat into the small hours until irrepressible yawns started circling the group and sleepiness overcame the men. One by one they fell to the messy floor and the sofas, and snores replaced words. Even the never-tired Old Brother dozed in an armchair. Only then did I really notice I was the sole female in the room and the man who sat next to me was the sole man who remained awake. When had he stopped talking? Over the loud buzzing of the floor fan, I turned to ask him for a cigarette, though I did not smoke. I held it in my mouth and he leaned over to give me a light from his. When the ends of the two cigarettes touched, I felt as if his breath and mine were threaded together, and I feared that a pair of eyes somewhere among the littered bodies might be peeking.

I drew on the cigarette hard but my lungs rejected the smoke. I tried to blow smoke rings but could shape nothing. All my efforts just resulted in a soggy cigarette. We sat there, no words, and did not look at each other. Our two chairs were like volcanic islands standing out among the sea of male bodies cluttering the floor. I suddenly felt naked and exposed. I stood up in panic and walked toward the door.

"Where can you go at this hour?" he said and frowned.

He was right; it was too late for me to go anywhere. Outside on the street the People's Militias were patrolling. Walking at this time of the night, I could be easily arrested as a female hooligan.

"Could you walk me home?" I asked.

"That would be even more dangerous."

So I sat down. He and I smoked in silence. In our two strings of smoke the window glass changed from gray to black then to gray again. From there it grew whiter and whiter. The pale yellow bulb in the room became fainter and fainter until I could no longer tell whether it was off or on. At last the entire chaos of the room was exposed clearly in the new daylight.

In the first rays of dawn I glanced at him. Thin smoke from his nose lingered on his pale face. The long sleepless night had painted dark rings around his eyes.

That night gained me a gang of new friends, though all were older, married men. Apparently the university girl who dared to sit overnight with those bare-shouldered men had won their affection. Their generation, the one that preceded mine, was a strange production of the Cultural Revolution. When they were about to graduate from middle school, all schools in China were closed. After a few years as Red Guards, they were sent to spend the better part of a decade in the countryside, either laboring in the fields, fooling around, or doing both. They received no more formal education; though many of them, especially those lucky enough to be inserted alongside erudite high school students, got the chance to read lots of "illegal books." They did many illegal things, including stealing and cheating for survival, besides reading illegal books. As a result, my new friends were a mix of wit, eclectic knowledge, and unusual survival skill. They were neither completely ignorant, nor fully educated. This signature of their generation was magnetic to me. I had also been in the countryside, but I was caught in a much later wave, got the chance to finish high school, and my "insertion" time was much shorter.

This age difference granted them the right to buy me nibbles and toys and to enjoy doing it. We went to movies together. On weekends, they brought me to sit in a teahouse all day long, leaving their wives and young children home. Around a square bamboo table, a covered teacup in front of each of us, we chatted about each other's real life stories. A waiter would come, carrying a tin teapot with a foot long spout, and refill our cups from a yard away. With a effortless wave of the teapot, a stream of hot water appeared from high in the air, then landed in the cup — no drop missing. Almost before a cup was filled, another stream was launched toward the next cup. I watched the waiter with amusement but the waiter never seemed to notice. I was always the only female in the teahouse; the glances from other "tea-guests" who played Chinese Chess or Go matches at nearby tables did not last long enough to bother me. It was in the noisiest teahouses that we found our most peaceful haven.

At the age of 25, I became a spoiled baby sister of these adoring big brothers, and happily tasted this belated teenage joy, ignoring approaching danger. One evening, the streets ablaze with colorful neon lights and crowded with pedestrians bumping elbows, Old Brother told me I was the only girl besides his wife with whom he went to movies. His face dimmed when he added that there could really be no friendship between a married man and an unmarried girl. It could be dangerous. Look, I immediately rebutted, this is a friendship between *one* girl and a *bunch* of men, what's so dangerous about that? When Old Brother was silent, I felt a sudden loss. Something, some innocent happiness had just evaporated. I gazed at the ground and kept walking. My unusual quietness led to their endless jokes; each of the men took a turn to try to make me smile. When they finally succeeded and the shadows were gone from my face, I caught the glances they exchanged among themselves, glances with an unconditional and tacit understanding that could only occur between men. Why couldn't we women have that? Why could I not share these mysteries with my female friends? Why was I not a man?

I sank into my own thoughts and did not notice the disappearance of the men, one after another. At last only three of us were left. Old Brother entrusted my "fortuneteller" to escort me home. "Don't be too serious," Old Brother warned before saying goodbye, though I wasn't sure that his advice was directed to me. It was advice I remembered often later, only when it was too late.

The two of us continued to stroll. "Fortuneteller" asked me why I always gave people the impression I was an orphan when I actually had a big family. His question made my nose tingle and eyes moist. I found I was telling him that every time I saw my younger sister, who was twenty, wrap her arms around our mother's neck and play the pampered child, I wondered why I was unable to do the same. I told him, perhaps my mother had given birth to me when she was too busy with revolutionary work, and I grew up so fast that she had no time for me. She followed the Party's doctrine that revolutionary work was more important than family. My younger sister only got lucky with mother's love because the shock of the Cultural Revolution had smashed mother's revolutionary will. I even told him that since I was a child, I received praise only when I brought home the highest grades, and willingly wore the patched clothes handed down from my older sister.

My outpouring of words was followed with silence. We walked on and then stopped to sit in a cold-drink store. He suddenly stood up and said in a low voice, "This is scary!" Before I was aware, he had hurried out. I stood watching his back disappear into a dense crowd.

That night I stayed awake for a long time and could not figure out why the pleasure of his company had turned to heaviness.

And the heaviness continued. The more we tried to maintain a rational friendship, the less our words made sense. I was almost unaware that we had stopped meeting the others in teahouses. We met, only the two of us, in his humble one-room apartment in a compound of indigent households. This was not his home. His home was in a distant suburb. He went home on weekends only.

My visits had started with lightness and pleasure. With each visit my fear of running into one of his neighbors increased.

"You know, I have a wife and a kid," he said one day. Until this point he had never mentioned his family. He was sitting on the edge of his bed, leaving the bamboo chair to me. The only other furniture in the room was a coat rack and a bamboo bookshelf full of old books. He did not seem to know where to put his hands; they kept moving from his lap to the edge of the bed then back to his lap. He said something, but I was not listening. His speech came out roughly with breath between them.

"I like you," I said. I had not thought of saying these words; they were said of themselves, without my knowing their exact meaning. All at once the street noise outside the window turned loud as thunder; inside the small room was dead silence.

His hands stilled. Then he stood up, slowly walked to the window. He stood there watching the busy traffic and the hurried pedestrians outside. I stared at his wide back, holding my head high.

He moved again. He walked to the closed door, each step echoing my heart beat. He grabbed the coat rack and started to shake it. The aged wooden rack made a cracking sound as if it could not bear his strength. He let go. Then he grabbed the iron door bolt and slid it back and forth, letting a vast echo of *Ping Ping Ping Ping* noise rub on my raw heart. I waited and said nothing, felt nothing. I was aware of my emptiness for the first time.

He stopped playing with the bolt and turned to face me, his gaze delirious and wild. Before I could react, he was standing over me. He pulled my face up with both hands and pressed his lips rudely on mine.

I closed my eyes, shivering. Within seconds, he erased all other men from my memory.

As I did not anticipate his sudden move, I did not anticipate his sudden cessation. *Is that it?* I opened my eyes confused.

"I have a wife and a kid," he said, almost inaudibly.

I walked out, my body rigid. The only sensation in me was the touch of his hands and lips. He had touched me.

The following weekend he didn't go home. In a suburban woods where no one else could see us, we sat shoulder to shoulder. At a pause of my own happy voice, I noticed that he seemed muted by something. At my next pause he had moved away from me a few inches. I continued talking and he moved a little more. When he stopped, he was more than a foot away. Puzzled, I stood up and walked over to him.

"No please," he said. His arms held his knees.

"What's the matter? Are you all right?"

"I'll be all right if you stay a foot away from me."

"Why? Are you not happy to be with me?"

"I am . . . my mind is . . . my body is not. . . ."

I stared at him, completely lost. That was when he started to laugh madly. "Are you really twenty-five?" He asked when his laughter finally came to a stop.

But I really hadn't any idea. My parents never talked about it, school never taught it, books never mentioned it, so where could I have gone to learn it?

This was what I had learned:

In the fourth year of my country life, my mother increased the frequency with which she wrote me, urging me to return to the city and take the job she had arranged along with her "backdoors" to make my return legal. I had witnessed the escape, through various legal and illegal channels, of almost all the city inserts. Old Brother had gone first. He was a man I respected. He never made fun of me although sometimes, meeting on a market day, he would look at me as if I were a lamb that had gone astray.

But my faith kept me in the village. I stayed in the country even after the Gang of Four, deemed the culprit of the disastrous Cultural Revolution, was arrested in October 1976, following Chairman Mao's death in September. My father contacted his old friend, the local county's Party Secretary, who came to my village himself with the mission to convince me to return home. I patiently explained to him my reasons for staying. As he was leaving he looked as if he did not know whether to laugh or cry. He, in turn, sent his subordinate, the district director whose jurisdiction included the commune of my village. Not wasting his saliva, he simply ordered me to go home.

That angered me. I asked him if I could make him believe my revolutionary determination by writing a vow with my own blood. He also left.

In desperation, my mother found a new weapon: a newspaper story about Zhu Kejia, a nationally publicized hard-working insert whom I sought to emulate as my role model. She clipped it out and sent it to me with a short note, "See for yourself, my daughter, that your worshipped Zhu Kejia is in jail now. He was a fake model made by the Gang of Four. He left the Kawa village long ago and had been doing politics in the provincial government yard all these years. Now, do you still want to root yourself in the country?"

I crumpled the letter, feeling numb for hours, and then cried behind my door.

From that day I stopped working in the fields, stopped teaching the night-school I had started for the peasants (not that they cared), and stopped talking to people. I neither returned to the city nor wrote letters home. I was in a trance when the news broke that the entrance exams for university would soon be given for the first time in eleven years.

For two months I buried myself in textbooks and scored number one on the exam for my district. I was admitted into the best university in the province. That's how I ran away from the village after those four long years. It was surprisingly easy to pull my feet out of the dirt there. Digging dirt, carrying pig manure, and eating sweet potatoes every meal. I did not miss it. Instead that whole existence became the source for prolonged new nightmares.

So that is how one's belief is broken.

From then on at home whenever a TV screen extolled the virtues of a communist martyr from *Before Liberation*, my younger sister and I would snicker while our mother wiped her tears. Five years my junior, my sister was a different generation. She laughed more than I. She had never gone to the countryside or held the belief that I had so painfully lost. I envy her, not burdened by a black hole in the heart.

It was more bothersome still when I realized that during the years of false belief I was more content. Which is better: to have a false belief and be content, or to break the false belief and feel empty?

Did my persistent pursuit of a higher purpose stagnate my sexual sense? Eight years after my false pregnancy from hugging a boy, my confusion remained.

One autumn night he wrote on his table calendar: "Could you please stay tonight?" It was past midnight and his walls were thin. I panicked. Unknown desire and a sense of danger hit me with hot and cold waves all at once. How would he do it? Exactly how would he do it to me?

"No." I wrote back.

"Yes!" He wrote.

"No!" I wrote again.

He tore the calendar page to pieces and pointed to the door. I wanted to kiss him good night but he pushed me away. For the first time he did not walk me home. I dragged myself through empty night streets in the cold wind all alone.

For several days we did not see each other, nor did we talk on the phone as usual. At work and at home my mind was occupied with only one thing. I must think it through before seeing him again. During these days the picture of a hanging lifeless body appeared in my mind more than once. In my college, a woman schoolmate hanged herself on a fourth floor window of our dorm, because she was pregnant by her boyfriend. She left a note to say she had no face, no will to live any more. I needed a reason for not killing myself, and for facing others.

I found an anatomy textbook in the city's public library and sat in a remote corner behind bookshelves to read it. All the time my face burned and my heart beat like a drum. Whenever someone passed by I covered the book with a newspaper. The book actually did not tell me directly what I was looking for. But my woman's instinct belatedly woke up as I stared at the picture of the naked male body with all the labels and arrows. At that point, I fell into a dilemma. Should I agree to his request? I had been told that an unbroken hymen was the most precious treasure. But why was it so precious? Because it was required to be unbroken when you marry? What if you loved someone you couldn't marry?

I then considered from a different angle. What would be the benefit of not giving myself to him? I would become a spinster. A spinster is another name for a crank. I didn't want to be a crank. Besides, an unbroken hymen would do no good to my physical health. I read in a Japanese novel that if a woman didn't get married by thirty, black spots would grow under her eyes. Where else had I also read that a woman's body would wither without a man?

That was how I convinced myself — love and health, two very good reasons.

What I did not expect was that it turned out to be so simple; so simple that I had not even had the time to feel anything. We spent our first night in a close friend's apartment, while she went to stay in a nearby hotel because a marriage certificate was required for a couple to share a room. We lay side by side on a bamboo mat, completely dressed and fully prepared to jump up at any minute, long after the dark, long after the human steps outside the door could no longer be heard.

So much for my precious hymen — it was pierced with just a pinch. A significant moment passed with no significant feeling. I knew, however, from this moment on, that things could never be reversed. Sadness overwhelmed me while my arms wrapped around his back and my breasts pressed tightly to his chest. When he finally turned on the light and saw fresh red spots on the mat, he seemed in a daze. He wanted to wipe up the blood but I was quicker to turn off the light. Our bodies were again intertwined as one and I soon forgot everything else. The last thing I remembered before falling into sleep was that he was still in me.

I woke up before dawn. Gray moonlight shed a long thin wedge through the slightly cracked curtains. I pulled the cool sheet up to cover my naked body and turned aside to look at his rough profile. He was soundly asleep. An immense satisfaction filled my heart.

"I love you," I whispered, wanting to say these unspeakable words before he woke.

"I love you too." He replied with such clarity, without opening eyes, that it startled me. It was the first — and also the last — time we said this to one another. In our dialect the word "love" has an embarrassing sound, and no sane person would speak it in daylight.

Years later in graduate school where I researched the depths of probability theory, after I had left him because he wouldn't divorce his wife for me, and after I had figured out that life, love and belief are all random events, I read an official English magazine published in Beijing. An article written by a Chinese graduate student, who shared a room with an international student, caught my eye. His roommate, a young American, couldn't understand why he had never slept with a girl.

In the article, the American student asked: "Don't you Chinese boys have any sexual desire at all?"

The Chinese student answered frankly: "Yes."

"Then how do you deal with it before marriage?"

The student gave the question some thought and said, "We endure it."

I showed this article to our English teacher, who was also from America. He shrugged and said he did not understand why China's population was so high if Chinese were so capable of enduring desire. #

SECOND ENCOUNTER

The building's shadow has shifted from west to east.

"George is running a little late," apologizes the interview coordinator, a Caucasian woman half a head taller than Wei Dong. The October afternoon sun glares through the window of this eighth floor office in Technology Square, next to MIT. Wei Dong eases back in the seat. It looks as if neither a rookie employee presenting a textbook question to test intelligence nor a mainlander who would not hesitate to lay an ambush for a fellow Chinese is in his way today. As a veteran software programmer, he has switched companies seven times in the past thirteen years, each moving him to a more challenging or better paying position — till this last time when he, along with his entire R&D group, was laid off. As good at interviews as he is, at this economic downturn, he dreads running into a countryman who has also gone through the baptism of the Cultural Revolution. "We Chinese are a plate of loose sand," he once grumbled to his wife after being stabbed in the back by a fellow Chinese. And once you are bitten by a snake, you can be startled by straw ropes for three years.

"Which part of China are you from?" The coordinator chats with Wei Dong as they wait for George.

"Sichuan." He mentions his province, but not his city. If he says Chongqing, he will have to spend too many lips and tongues in explanation. Nobody here seems to know Chongqing, even though it was once the capital of China during the Japanese invasion.

"I know Sichuan," the lady says, "the spicy food!"

"That's right," Wei Dong nods politely. In America, the sole impression of his home, his beautiful and painful home, is its food. "Spicy food with no fortune cookies," he adds.

"That's what George said. You know, George is also . . ."

A knock on the door, a head with black hair cranes in. "Speak of the devil," the coordinator smiles. "This is our Principal Engineer, George Zhang." Wei Dong stands up while his heart sinks at the introduction. The lady, like most Americans, can't pronounce a Chinese 'Z' properly. But that merely highlights the real problem: Only a mainland Chinese could have such a surname. In Taiwan or Hong Kong, the surname would be "Chang" instead. The short man at the door looks about the same age as Wei Dong, with the same yellow skin — what kind of Chinese is he to use a foreign given name? No doubt one with the potential to demolish Wei Dong's opportunity.

The new interviewer has Wei Dong's résumé in hand. He scrutinizes Wei Dong's face, forcing a nod from the latter. The scrutiny is too intense for an interview. An eerie sensation washes down Wei Dong's body, and he is startled by Zhang's exclamation: "Wei Dong! It really is you! Do you remember me?" He waves Wei Dong's résumé as if it is a witness.

Wei Dong narrows his eyes slightly; his gaze dwells on Zhang's ordinary and energetic face for a moment. Then he shakes his head. "Sorry, no." Both men are speaking English, and Wei Dong detects a southern Chinese accent in the other man's speech, just like his own.

Zhang whispers to the coordinator and the latter nods several times. Wei Dong cannot make out his words, and Zhang's intimacy with a white woman bothers him. The good mood is broken. It is not a good omen that a man whom he doesn't know claims to have known him.

Zhang escorts Wei Dong from the coordinator's room, and leads him toward his office. He stops halfway and asks again, "Do you really not remember me?" This time he speaks in Chinese.

"Sorry, I still don't. Where do we know each other from?" Wei Dong answers in Chinese as well. It sounds funny when he says "sorry" in Chinese, as it is not an expression used in the daily dialogue of his hometown. Disappointment sweeps through Zhang's face and he sighs a philosopher's sigh, "I'm not surprised. One remembers what one wants to remember."

He now speaks in Chongqing dialect.

"When did you come to America?" Wei Dong asks, curiosity and alarm rising together.

"You want to know? Hey, let's go to a Sichuan restaurant and have a cup! How's that?" His enthusiasm is typically Chongqing, a characteristic of those raised on hot peppers and relentless gray winters. The enthusiasm affects Wei Dong. He has not had a drinking partner for a while, and drinking is no fun without a partner and Sichuan dishes.

"What about my interview?"

"You are done! I'm the last one on your list," Zhang says.

"Where are we going?"

"Chinatown, of course, unless you want to go for fake Chinese food."

Striding across the sparsely filled parking lot, Wei Dong pictures its past crowdedness. They get into Zhang's gold Camry and drive across the Charles River. Luckily, there is an open meter on the small street next to South Station, the main train and bus interchange for Boston. They walk along Kneeland Street. Near the off-ramp of the Mass Pike stands a bearded, stocky white man in T-shirt, waving a cardboard sign to passing cars: "WILL WORK FOR MONEY."

"What are you looking at?" Zhang asks.

Out of habit, Wei Dong is looking up at a five-floor beige stone building across the intersection. Chinatown is not an intimate or attractive place to him; he comes here only when his wife needs native groceries that she can't get in Stop & Shop or Bread & Circus. However this building is an exception. On its flat top, a red-pillared, green-tiled pavilion with eight flying eaves is visible. He always looks at it when he comes here; it makes him homesick. In Sichuan this type of pavilion is common, though never on top of a building. He had thought to build such a pavilion himself in the yard of his new house, but that was before he was laid off. Now he doesn't know if he'll be able to keep paying the mortgage.

Today, something else catches his eye. On the south side of the building, facing the Mass Pike off-ramp, the relief characters "Welcome to Chinatown" have been covered with a long red silk banner fluttering in the autumn wind. On the banner are bold words written in both Chinese and English:

天 佑 美 国

GOD BLESS AMERICA

This red banner was not there before September 11. Wei Dong stares at the Chinese line. Unlike the English slogan, which seems complacent, the Chinese words beg for blessing and protection. Something warm rolls inside his throat. Zhang follows his eyes. They speak no words for a moment, then resume their walk.

Across the packed streets smelling of roasted duck, smoking oyster sauce, and live fish, Zhang takes Wei Dong to a restaurant named "Old Sichuan," half empty this afternoon. The scent of ginger and scallions supplants the outside odors. The hostess, a young girl, apparently knows Zhang. "Which good wind blows you here?" she says in Mandarin, trying to make it sound like Sichuanese, and deftly sets a table with Chinese zodiac placemats for two.

"What'd you like to drink, Mr. Zhang?" the girl asks sweetly.

"Guizhou Maotai! Do you have it?"

"Mr. Zhang, what happiness are you celebrating?" the talkative girl asks. Wei Dong scrunches his eyebrows a little: a bottle of Maotai would only be opened on an important occasion.

"I met my savior today," Zhang points to Wei Dong. "We must have Maotai. Give us your finest wine cups!"

Wei Dong is now certain that this townsman of his has it all wrong. He might have ended a life when he was a teenager but he had most definitely never saved one.

"Townsman," Wei Dong says, "that's not the reason for the celebration. I'm surely not your savior. But I'll be happy to hear your story and celebrate our meeting today."

"Sit down, sit down. I know what I'm talking about. It's my treat today." Zhang orders cold dishes first. *Tingling and Hot Beef Stomach. Garlic Seaweed. Red-oil Three Slices.* He then orders hot dishes. *Twice Cooked Pork. Quick-fried Tripe. Broad-Bean Sauce Silver Carp.* All are the familiar spicy dishes that Wei Dong associates with his motherland.

"Too much," says Wei Dong.

Zhang raises his hand to counter Wei Dong's objection, pours the hard liquor in their delicate, white-blue China wine cups, and holds up his cup: "Gan!"

Wei Dong covers his cup with a palm. "Townsman," he says, "I'm a forthright man who does not drink insinuative wine. First tell me why you think we knew each other."

"Dry this cup up and I'll tell you."

"Doable."

They both drink and show the other the bottom of the cup.

"1968. How many years ago was that?"

"Thirty-three." It was the year when the *armed fighting* between two factions of Red Guards was at its peak. Each faction believed its interpretation of Mao's revolutionary line was the pure and correct one, and that the others were villains.

"Thirty-three years ago, you were a student of the Secondary School attached to the Southwest Normal University, right?"

"Yes," Wei Dong feels goosebumps on his back. This information is not on his résumé. But he is not convinced that this man really knew him personally. He was a Red Guard faction leader then; many Chongqing people from that time might know his name. He has an impulse to stop this man's reminiscence, but he restrains himself.

"You were the head of 'Spring Thunder.' "

"True." Wei Dong says as calmly as he can. "Spring Thunder" was an armed fighting team of his Red Guard faction.

"In the summer of 1968, you commanded an armed fight against us, '8.31.' And you won. You captured the Library Building we occupied, and took several of us prisoners."

"Were you among those?"

"Unfortunately, yes."

Wei Dong looks at Zhang again carefully, and still doesn't find anything familiar.

"Your people wanted to execute us," Zhang says.

"You killed one of our fighters." Through the gunpowder smoke diluted by time, Wei Dong can still see the specter of a body wrapped in white sheets, lying motionless on the ground. Fierce faces and guns swinging around in syncopation with the outcry: "Blood debts must be paid in blood!"

"Not me personally. But maybe. Probably." Zhang downs another cup of the intense liquor. His face starts to show redness, a sign that he is upset or can't hold his drink.

"Revenge was the sentiment then."

"Maybe. So you said, 'Just one! One for one!'"

Wei Dong nods slowly. He might have said that. He was a leader known for being accurate on numbers. His math was the best in class before the Cultural Revolution.

"And someone pulled me out and covered my eyes," Zhang says.

Wei Dong sees a remote figure in his wine cup, a short young man in a sleeveless singlet, hands tied behind his back, eyes covered by a dirty rag, face blackened by smoke; this may explain why he couldn't recall anything familiar about Zhang. "I fuck your ancestor!" the blindfolded young man had cursed at the top of his lungs. "I fight for Chairman Mao! I die for Chairman Mao! Shoot me! Get it done quick!"

Zhang continues, "I kept shouting because waiting to die was the scariest thing," he smiles bitterly and keeps drinking. "Through all my shouting, though, I could still hear the trigger being pulled."

Wei Dong awaits his account. His hand, holding the empty wine cup, is steady.

Zhang suddenly laughs. He points to Wei Dong. His laughter makes him choke and he is out of breath as he blurts out: "It was . . . it was . . . a dud. . . ."

"Go on," Wei Dong fills Zhang's cup with more Maotai, and also fills his own.

"The shooter was angry and yelled, 'Fuck! Let me do it again!' I could feel the barrel aiming at my face and — no point in concealing it from you now — my pants were wet." A wry grin passes a corner of Zhang's mouth. "Then you said, 'Shit gun! Save your bullet for the next fight. It's his damn luck.' And you let me go."

Zhang pauses. Wei Dong looks to the nearby tables. The table on their left is empty; on their right three men speak incomprehensible Cantonese in loud voices.

"So you are my savior. But why? Why'd you let me go?" Zhang's hard stare forces Wei Dong to face him.

Wei Dong remembers that fight, but doesn't remember all the details. He was only a 14-year-old boy then. What Zhang describes surely is like what he would have done. Wei Dong's father, a professional military officer, had been very superstitious. He had told his impressionable son that a misfire is an inauspicious sign for a shooter; it means that the enemy has not reached the end of his life yet and must be let go. Otherwise, it would bring misfortune to the shooter. If that was what Wei Dong did, it was the only thing he did that had not been in the name of revolution during that time.

He does not tell Zhang this. He asks, "Did we . . . shoot anyone else after we let you go?"

"Don't know. As soon as I got out of the Library Building I never wanted to be a Red Guard again."

"Good for you," Wei Dong clinks his glass with Zhang's and takes a sip. He had stayed in his faction of Red Guard a lot longer, until Chairman Mao no longer needed them and sent them to the countryside for re-education by poor peasants.

The whole-fish covered with starchy brown sauce and scallions arrives as the last dish, giving off aromatic steam. Zhang jabs his chopsticks into it, and takes a fluffy white morsel to his mouth. "Mmm," he says, "The cook is not bad. Not bad at all. Eat." He puts a piece in Wei Dong's bowl.

The subject changes. They talk about names they both knew from their Red Guard times. Some of their acquaintances had been executed by the government after the Cultural Revolution. Some are now rich businessmen in the mainland. There were many people they had both known during the Cultural Revolution, save Chairman Mao the Great Leader himself. Neither of the once loyal Red Guard had ever seen him with their own eyes or heard his words directly. They do not bother to mention what had made them enemies thirty-three years ago.

They talk about their teenage sons and the games the kids like to play. *Tomb Raider. Resident Evil.* They spill out these names almost simultaneously, pausing, then laughing at the coincidence. "It's good that they shoot the screen," says Zhang.

"I hope they don't treat reality as a screen," says Wei Dong.

"This is a time, and that was another." Zhang's tongue is enlarged by alcohol.

They drink and talk like two old friends who haven't seen each other for a long, long time. By the end of the dinner, Zhang is as drunk as mud and in no condition to drive. Wei Dong is not drunk. He is merely satisfied that his capacity is no less than when he was young, probably the only heroic valor that remains with him. He orders a pot of very thick tea, and drinks two full cups in an attempt to neutralize the effects of the alcohol. On the table littered with plates and bowls, the dishes on his side are nearly untouched.

He takes the keys from Zhang's pocket, pays for the dinner, and goes to the gold Camry. When he drives Zhang's car back to the front door of "Old Sichuan," the girl at the front desk and another waiter are holding Zhang up. They help load him into the car. Wei Dong drives to Technology Square, parks Zhang's car, and moves Zhang into his own silver Camry.

His car glides quietly in the dark along the Mass Pike with Zhang snoring in the back seat. For a moment he worries that Zhang, the ordinary townsman who reminds him nothing at all of the irreconcilable enemy from decades ago, might puke in his well-maintained interior. Outside, the sound of traffic washes over his window like an ocean tide. Streams of red taillights stretch to the invisible fore; behind him endless white headlights keep coming from unseen origins. On the car radio the 1030 News Station talks about the unsure signs of economic recovery, lingering terrorist threats, a shooting at an abortion clinic, and suicide bombers in Israel.

Wei Dong's hands sweat cold, moistening the steering wheel. The killing, all of it, was done in the name of God, or one revered as God, for whom his blood once boiled. It's frightening to relate those feverish fanatics to his remote self of thirty-three years ago. What was heroic, just, and glorious then, is ignorant, criminal, and shameful now. It seems only those who survive the waste can understand, dooming new generations to repeat it in different places, for different causes.

He still is unsure if he killed anyone in those "armed fights" in Chongqing, though he knew he had opened fire in battles. "Bullets don't grow eyes," his father often had said.

He doesn't want to think about it further. Hopefully tomorrow morning Zhang won't consider ruining his employment opportunity. He is a skilled software developer who deserves the position. He has made Boston his home and he needs to keep paying for the new house that he, his wife and son love.

In a western suburb of Boston, his wife opens the door and starts. "Why are you home so late? What happened? Who is this?" she asks in an alarmed, rapid Chongqing dialect.

"An eternal friend from the old time," Wei Dong replies. "Help me to get him in." #

Xujun Eberlein grew up in Chongqing, China, moved to
the United States in 1988, and holds a Ph.D. from MIT.
An award-wining writer, she lives with her husband and
daughter in Wayland, Massachusetts. Xujun can be reached
through her website, www.xujuneberlein.com.